OLLIE'S TEST

Book One of Ollie's Heart

Mark Mortland

7th Street Dreams

DISCLAIMER

Ollie's Test is a work of fiction intended for mature audiences. It contains themes of self-discovery, personal growth, and romantic intimacy between consenting adults. While this story explores emotional and physical relationships, it is a work of fiction and should not be interpreted as a depiction of real events or individuals.

All characters are fictional and over the age of 18. Any similarities to real persons, living or deceased, are purely coincidental. This book contains themes related to LGBTQ+ identity, emotional trauma, and overcoming personal struggles. While the story is written with sensitivity and care, reader discretion is advised.

Additionally, the medical situations depicted in this book are fictionalized for storytelling purposes and should not be considered professional advice. If you or someone you know is facing a similar situation, please seek guidance from a qualified professional.

The author does not condone discrimination, hate, or harmful behaviors of any kind. This story is ultimately about love, trust, and finding the strength to move forward.

TABLE OF CONTENTS

CHAPTER 1: ALONE AND SURVIVING

I was alone.

And anxious, in the truest sense. With a respectable amount of 'nervous' - plus a bit of good old-fashioned 'terrified' thrown in for fun. Not to mention about twenty other uncomfortable emotions I couldn't even name. Life had been teaching me plenty of lessons lately, and this upcoming medical exam wasn't making my world any more manageable. But, hey, it was just one more test I needed to pass.

Recently, I literally started peeing my pants at work - which, believe me, was a major freak-out moment. After my initial panic died down, the embarrassment hit. Imagine standing up from the conference room table after an hour-long meeting only to realize your pants were soaked. My mild urge to go to the bathroom had felt manageable, like something I could easily hold until after our meeting. Having an "accident" isn't exactly normal for a nineteen-year-old trying to make a good impression on his coworkers.

I was the "kid" on my team, a first-time co-op student a little over three months into my spring and summer terms. My co-workers took great pride and delight in acting as my surrogate parents. Honestly, I needed their attention and guidance, so I welcomed it. They never once made me feel ashamed. In fact, they gave me lots of much-needed reassuring hugs. Well, *careful* hugs - they didn't wanna risk getting wet as well - but hugs all the same.

Most importantly, my co-op mentor, Ted, had a good friend who was a urologist and was willing to see me right away - without me first having to get a referral from a primary care physician. Ted called in the favor himself, and when I asked why he'd go so out of his way, he warmly said, "That's what mentors are for Sport." Believe me, I had zero clue how any of this medical stuff worked, so I was just relieved to get help.

Not only did Ted go out of his way for me, but the urologist turned out to be one of the nicest "dad"-types

I had ever met. His name was Dr. Rainer, but he insisted I call him Chris. From the moment we met, he had a calming presence about him - like nothing I said could faze him. He just sat there, listening to my story with the kind of empathy that made me forget I was talking about something so embarrassing. There was no judgment. No awkward questions. Just kindness and encouragement. And for the first time in weeks, I felt like I wasn't completely alone in all this.

Chris agreed that a healthy, athletic kid shouldn't be wetting his business-casual attire. After ruling out a simple bladder infection, he recommended we immediately schedule a special urology test. He warned me it was a bit "involved," repeating words like "intimate" and "exposed" in a way that sounded less clinical and more, well... *ominous*. I had no idea what it really meant, but I guess I was about to find out. Because...

... Here I was in a strip mall parking lot in Rockwall on a Thursday evening, staring at a row of medical "storefronts." Wait... Were those even the correct terms? I mean, this wasn't a mall, and those businesses definitely weren't stores - just a line of foreboding entrances that seemed to get gloomier the longer I contemplated them. Naturally, the urology clinic I was destined for turned out to be the most forlorn of them all. *Perfect.*

I worked on the other side of this huge, sprawling metroplex, a good ninety-minute drive away, even without traffic. My appointment was tomorrow at *eight in the morning* - on a Friday no less. There was no way I could make it here on time, especially with rain in the forecast.

I wasn't usually a Type A perfectionist, except when it came to being punctual. Even the *thought* of showing up late tightened my chest like a vice. Considering stress was a big part of my problem - according to Dr. Rainer - it seemed counterproductive to let it spiral out of control. So yeah... I was about to spend the night in my bright blue Bronco in a nearby parking lot to guarantee I showed up on time because *that* wasn't stressful at all.

After I memorized the clinic's location, I left to find a cozy, well-lit sleeping spot in the nearest mega-Walmart parking lot. Texas didn't seem to have a shortage of those. Please believe me, I was grateful. I've learned the hard way about choosing the *wrong* place to park in for the night.

****

Against all odds, I actually slept through the whole night. No one tapped on my windows, no threatening shadows loomed over my sleeping form, and I woke up safe and sound. I'd parked between three RVs, like a circle of sleepy guardians; just happy families taking a break from the interstate. The night was quiet, uneventful, and precisely what I needed.

Unfortunately, while Walmart restrooms were awesome, their employees tended to get suspicious when you started brushing your teeth and changing clothes in them. I got it - they had to draw the line somewhere, and while I totally appreciated their parking-lot hospitality, I didn't want to overstay my welcome.

This morning, my pits were a little, well, *aromatic.* I was completely out of deodorant. Truth be told, I kinda liked my smell. It reminded me of when I was a kid and my father would come home from work. He'd scoop me up into a big hug, and I'd bury my face in his chest near his pit. I can't quite express it, but he was like the scent of comfort, safety, and *love.* Things I desperately longed for right now.

Anyway, enough reminiscing. I didn't know much about this test. Just what I'd already said: it was going to be *intimate.* And that I'd be, er, *exposed.* So, I needed to freshen up as much as possible. Lucky for me, there was a Buc-ee's right across the interstate. Truck-stop restrooms were perfect for folks starting their morning routines on the road - nobody even bats an eye.

I topped off my tank to justify using their facilities, grabbed my fresh shirt on its hanger, and headed in. No one even gave me a second glance. After brushing my teeth and wetting my hair - which didn't help much with my curls, but hey, I didn't want to look homeless. I washed my face, then ducked into an open stall with a few damp paper towels to wipe down my pits, crotch, and butt crack.

When I exited and returned to my Bronco with my fresh shirt and undies on, I was as prepared as I could get. As long as I didn't start sweating, I was golden. Well, maybe just bronze, but I'd take it.

CHAPTER 2: GO TIME

Go Time was here. It was 7:50, "The Test" was in ten minutes, and I had to admit, I was just stalling here in my Bronco outside the medical storefronts, watching patients shuffle in. I feared I was finally beginning to look a little creepy, so I stepped out - took a deep breath - and pushed myself through the door. Hey! Inside, it was surprisingly normal, and not nearly as scary or sketchy as it looked from the parking lot. It was just a standard waiting room with a reception desk behind an obviously improvised COVID window.

Except every other guy in here was *ancient.* I understood that thirty, or even forty, was still pretty young. But, these men were in their seventies or eighties - maybe some were only in their fifties or sixties - but all were clearly uncomfortable, if not in outright pain. I felt a pang of guilt: I needed to just forget my stupid fears; I mean, *why was I even here?* They were the ones who genuinely needed help.

Almost like an epiphany, I was hit by the urge to slip back out, climb back into my Bronco, and quickly drive away. Until the desk lady noticed my trepidation and honed right in: "Baby, it's okay." Yes, she actually said *Baby* as she motioned me over. I caved. I didn't cry, but it was a close thing. Instead, I accepted her estimation, took a shaky breath, and walked over to her window.

"Hi, I'm Ollie. Er, Oliver, ah Oliver Carson. I'm here for a procedure, I mean test, at eight." I blurted out a final, "I'm sorry." Lurd, why did I say I was I sorry? But I swear I was. Just shoot me.

Thankfully, she kindly gave me the sweetest smile - no laughter, just pure comfort. She had no idea how much I needed that, but then again, I probably made it all too clear exactly how much I did.

She confirmed my appointment and informed me that my absolutely incredible, amazing, godsend insurance plan had taken care of everything except for $25. I'd lost the coverage I had from my parents, but being a co-op student had its benefits. *So, thank you, big Government Contractor Company for gifting me those lost benefits. I never expected I'd have to use them, but you never know how much something means until you need it.*

After a few more clicks on her keyboard, she gave me a final warm smile. "Everything looks good. I see you've already filled out all your new patient forms online - thank you; that makes my job so much easier. Just have a seat, baby boy, and **Corey** will call you back as soon as we're ready."

Baby boy? Dang it. *I'm not blushing - you are.* I mumbled a quick "Thanks" and searched for a chair as far away from all the "serious" patients as I could find.

Wait - did she say "Corey" or maybe "Cora?" No... defin-itely Corey. Oh frak. I'd somehow made my mind up that the person doing my test would be some sweet elderly lady. *Could "Corey" be an old lady's name? Names can go both ways, right? Pat, Riley, Tony, Dana...*

Please, please, please don't let "Corey" be a *he.*

And absolutely do *not* let "Corey" be cute.

I squirmed in my chair, trying not to sweat too much. Unfortunately, that was my family's super-power: my father always joked that we're "big, blond furry sweaters." I wasn't sure I was *big* exactly, but dang, did we ever sweat at the first sign of stress or hint of exercise.

I also couldn't deny my physical resemblance to my father. We both had soft, loose blond curls, though mine might be a shade lighter. My calves, thighs, and tummy also sported a decent amount of blond fur, and I as-sumed he had a comparably furry butt crack, though that *definitely* wasn't something I'd ever seen since pu-berty. And I was hoping that my new little center patch of blond chest hair would eventually take over my pecs - pit to pit, and neck to nipples - just like his had done.

Then there was my scruffy blond beard. My father called it my "baby-beard." He constantly begged me to never shave it so he could watch it fill in as I grew up. But that was back when he still talked to me. *Stop it!* I couldn't afford to think about that right now. I had made it here on my own, and I was fine. At least until...

A man I assumed had to be Corey stepped out from

a doorway and called my name. *Frak.* I was so totally-*frakked.* Oh my *lurd.* (I said "lurd" and "frak" because they were made-up words and my family was very religious. Even after everything, I still tried to respect that). But honestly, this Corey person was my *frakkin' perfect man.* I stood up, and he offered me his hand - politely ignoring my uncontrolled, hero-worshipping, deer-in-the-headlights gawk. After an eternity, I finally realized that I should probably maybe *shake* it in return, and that's when I noticed that he was even taller than my own 6'3" stature.

Dangit! I was just trying to get through all this with minimal embarrassment. So, of course, Corey had to be a 6'5" tower of muscle - basically my kryptonite. Guessing ages wasn't my strong suit, but I was thinking he's maybe about thirty (the age that absolutely did me in). He had a slightly rugged but absolutely beautiful face with a sweet, still boy-like smile. Most importantly - right now, anyway - he had the kindest sky-blue eyes I'd ever seen. Which was good because *I needed all the reassurance I could get.*

He could practically be my father's hot younger brother. Same dark-blond hair - only straight - a full beard, and, if that bit of chest fur poking out of his scrubs was any indication, he was rocking my father's furry chest gene. *I was doomed.*

So here I stood, facing the single most stunningly gorgeous man I could imagine, who just emerged from "the door" to escort me into "the room" to administer "the test." Again, as I had been warned, it was pretty much the most *intimate* test ever. Why do doctors say "intimate" like it's some polite euphemism? Why not call it what it is: embarrassing and, most likely, humiliating?

CHAPTER 3: AN INTIMATE INTRODUCTION

I finally realized I'd just been standing there, awkwardly anchored in place. Corey graciously broke the spell by saying, "You're a good-looking young man, and I'm sure your body is something to be proud of. But I think you'd be more comfortable getting undressed - *if* we headed to our room." Then he gave me the sweetest, most inviting smile - enough to unfreeze my legs. As we walked back through the door, he politely added, "I'm Corey, your nurse."

"Hi, I'm Ollie," I said, walking beside him down a not-very-welcoming hallway.

Corey glanced over. "I kind of figured that when you stood up after I called 'Oliver.'" He flashed a mischievous grin and patted my shoulder. "But it's nice to know you go by 'Ollie.' We're going to that last room on the right."

I blushed - or maybe went pale; I couldn't be sure - and dropped my gaze. "Yeah, sorry," I mumbled. "I guess I'm just... nervous."

He only smiled, sliding his hand down my shoulder to the small of my back, gently guiding me into a room that was bigger than I'd expected. "Here's our home for the next 90 minutes, *Ollie*. So, take a deep breath and relax."

Relax? In this room? *Sure!*

First off, on the left wall, there was The Chair, or more precisely, *the Chair-Table of Bizarre Medical Experiments*, currently configured in a very upright position, complete with split padded leg rests and restraints. Adding to its ambiance of wrongness, there was a funnel hanging from it on a nylon cord, with a hose attached leading down into a plastic container that looked kinda like an old-fashioned plastic milk carton, except it had measurement lines on its side.

The wall opposite the chair-table had a large sink on its right, bristling with enough disturbing, vaguely-medical-looking equipment to make me glance away fast. And a collection of things no man should have to see on the left. I mean, I *thought* I knew what a catheter looked like or what I *imagined* them to look like. But why were there like 20 of them just hanging there on the wall and how can they be so long? And what were those things next to them that looked like - Lurd! - dildos on a cord?

Not to be outdone, the far wall had its horrors as well. There was a stationary flat exam table. That was perfectly fine, but why was there a toilet? And why was it just plopped right there, right out in the open without anything to protect a user's modesty? This time, I know

I paled; I even got a little nauseated. I really should have eaten something last night or this morning.

Corey quickly picked up on my color drain and eased me into a normal-looking chair by the door. I hadn't even noticed it during my panicked survey of the room. Grateful for his kindness, I sat down and tried not to let any tears leave my eyes.

"Hey, Ollie. It's okay," he said reassuringly. "I'm here to help you. Think of me as your best friend - or big brother - for the next 90 minutes. I promise I'll guide you through everything, and we'll be fine. Okay?"

All I could do was nod, not trusting my voice at the moment.

Corey rubbed between my shoulders and gave me a second questioning "*Okay*?" Then he gently placed his warm hand on the top of my head before sliding it down to cup my almost furry cheek, making me raise my eyes to meet his reassuring gaze.

"Okay," I managed, trying to sound like I believed it - as I looked into his eyes, maybe, just maybe, I kinda did.

"Let's start with the basics," he said reassuringly. "What did your urologist tell you about a urodynamic flow study?"

"Well, he mostly just stressed that it's very... *intimate*. He explained that I'd have to pee while I'm hooked up to some monitors that measure how well my bladder and pelvic muscles work together. And he warned me I'd be pretty exposed."

Corey gave a soft chuckle. "Well... That's a very high-level, *detail-free* way of putting it. But don't worry - like I said, I've got you. Before I get into all the gory details of the *actual* procedure, can you tell me what happened that made your doctor send you here?"

I broke eye contact and looked down at the floor again. "About a month ago, I accidentally got into a fight with a couple of strangers. I was in the wrong place at the wrong time. They managed to land some solid hits to my abdomen and kidney areas before I convinced them I wasn't giving up easily."

I sighed, deciding to just lay it all out. "After that, my bathroom habits changed. I started needing to go a lot more often, but it was like I'd barely dribble a little each time I went. I blew it off. Until one day at work, I looked down after a long meeting and discovered that I'd wet my pants. My coworkers decided that was enough and helped me find you."

I looked back up, unsure what I'd find in Corey's expression. Instead of judgment, I saw genuine concern. "I'm sorry, Ollie," he said caringly. "That's awful. Are your parents close enough to help you through all this?"

I hadn't braced for a question like that; my usual defenses faltered, and a single tear escaped before I could stop it. "No, they're in Michigan. Listen... I'm sorry. I swear I was going to tell you this before we started anyway. I'm, um... I'm gay. And I figured that getting my first real job and moving away from home to a new city was the perfect time to come out to them. They disagreed - *big time*. My father let me keep my clothes, my Bronco, and my phone - while I'm away from school. But otherwise, I'm on my own. They never want to see me again and they won't answer my calls. So no, they're not close, and I guess they don't care what happened."

Corey's face fell, burdened with grief-stricken sympathy. "First off, we'll talk about your parents - and about you being away from school - later. But, Ollie, there's nothing you need to apologize for. Not about this test, not about anything. You're okay; I'm here for you."

He paused, letting his reassurance sink in, then added, "Also, on a lighter note, you didn't need to tell me you're gay." His eyes gleamed mischievously. "I pretty instantly picked up on that back in the waiting room. Has anyone told you that you have a terrible poker face?" He sent me a quick grin. "But for the record, I was flattered." He gave me a slight nod of appreciation - as a friendly joke - I was sure.

I was relieved by his honesty but wasn't entirely comfortable with him just yet. I needed to state my concerns clearly. "Well, the problem is, I tend to get... um, well, I usually can't *contain my excitement,* even during normal medical exams. My pediatrician would simply brush it off - because it happened every time I saw him, and he just got used to it - but I was always mortified. Now, with Dr. Rainer telling me how *intimate* this test is, I thought I should warn you in case I, you know, embarrass myself... and *then* you found out I was gay."

Corey let out an easy laugh. "You've gotta let some of your anxiety go, buddy," he said, giving my shoulder a reassuring squeeze. "Nothing that's about to happen will upset me, and it *shouldn't* upset you either. Think of it like this: I'm effectively going to be in control of your body, like when a doctor taps your knee with that little rubber hammer. If your knee *doesn't* jerk, we know something's wrong. If you *don't* express what you politely call your 'excitement' during certain parts of this test, *I'll* be worried."

Pausing again, he looked into my eyes, making sure his reassurances were getting through to me. "And finally, Ollie, I'm a nurse. I have a penis, and I see a lot of other guys' penises too. I know how they work - and what they do when you least expect or *want* it. We nurses are used to it. Our main concern is making sure *you* feel okay about it."

Then I noticed a bright glint in his eye, and he casually added, "Oh, and I'm gay too."

I suddenly I had a very nonplussed look on my face.

"Ha! I love it," Corey teased. "Look at that face. You really do need to be more open about showing your emotions." He chuckled. "What? Did you think you were the only big, beefy, bearded - well, *almost* bearded for you - guy who's gay?" And there it was again, that half-smile-smirk telling me he wasn't laughing *at* me. Instead, I believe he's working really hard to connect *with* me.

I blushed, trying - and failing - *not* to show how much I was instantly crushing on him. He winked. "Look, I know I just gave you the 'I'm a medical professional' speech, but you deserve a little unprofessionalism." He tugged me up from the chair and wrapped me in a big ol' bear hug.

Wow. I hadn't realized how badly I needed that. I let myself sink into his arms, nuzzling against his chest, as a couple more tears slipped free - tears of relief I didn't even know I'd been holding back.

CHAPTER 4: ARE YOU KIDDING ME

I quickly realized that Corey's scent reminded me of my father's love and safety and I had to leave his comforting embrace maybe a little too quickly. Hopefully he just thought it was time to end our hug. Lurd though! I could have stayed wrapped in his arms for the whole ninety minutes. As I stepped away, Corey crossed to the door, shutting it with a soft click. Once again, Go Time was here.

"Okay Ollie, just a few quick basic questions, then we'll get to the fun stuff," he said, turning back to me. "You're nineteen, right?"

"Yes. But I'll be twenty in a little over three months."

"Got it. And you're six-foot-three and weigh around one-seventy-five?"

"Yeah, I'm trying hard to bulk up a bit more though."

Corey seemed to appraise my build before he continued, "Any allergies to latex or rubber?"

"Um... Not that I know of?"

"Perfect! Now before you undress, let me give you the

plan." He gave me a playful wink, "*You know*, all those gory details your urologist accidently left out." I barely saw a cute little smirk before he realized he must have forgotten something, "Oh, wait! You remembered to show up with a full bladder and didn't drink anything with caffeine yesterday or this morning, right?"

"Yes, sir!"

He let out a short laugh. "Wow, a genuine 'Yes, sir.' Your father's a fool for pushing you away." Then he caught himself, shrugging apologetically. "Sorry, we can talk about all that later. For your first task: I'll need you to pee into that funnel and empty your bladder as much as you can. Are you pee-shy at all?"

I felt comfortable enough that I grinned and replied, "I was on the football team all through high school. You learn how to pee with the whole team by your side. I'm good."

"Great!" Corey returned my smile, "then I'll just stay here in the room with you. After that, you'll need to get undressed. And I recommend completely. It's just me in here and believe me, I'm going to see everything you've got anyway. This test involves a lot of peeing and let's just say it doesn't always go where you expect it to - better safe and dry than sorry."

Corey once again immediately noticed my moderately shocked reaction, but continued.

"So, Ollie my man, please don't freak out about the next part. It's hopefully where you first show some 'excitement.'" He gave me a playful grin, "I'm going to get you up on that far table and give you a very 'intimate' rectal and prostate exam. I'll explain why as we go."

He chuckled when he noticed my cheeks reddening. "Hey, there it is! That's what I want to see! Too much blood in your cheeks is way better than not enough. No more going pale and making me worry you might pass out."

I saw a playful smirk, "There *may* be a couple of surprise steps after that. Hey, I gotta keep some mystery in our morning, right?" Another wink. "But no matter what, the next task is likely to be the least *exciting* part. I'll do an 'in-and-out' catheter to see how much urine is still left in your bladder after you pee."

Then he pointed to the wall left of the sink. "After that, the next likely *exciting* step involves those things you see hanging there beside the regular catheters. They're anal catheter-probe sensors. I'll be inserting one into your rectum, placing it so that it gently nuzzles against your prostate. I'll also have to put two ECG-style electrodes on either side of your anus and tape it all up to keep everything in place"

Dumbfounded, I could only stare at him, wearing my best *You're kidding, right?* expression. If Corey noticed, he didn't seem surprised - as if he'd given this exact speech a hundred times before and I was just following his well-rehearsed script.

"Hey, it's okay - just keep those cheeks nice and red." Corey grinned. "The electrodes won't send any current into your body, they just measure how and when your anal muscles move."

"After that, we jump right back to another *boner-killer*: I'll insert a thinner, but stiffer, catheter into your bladder again, and this time we'll slowly *fill* it with saline. I have to tape it in place as well. We'll have plenty of time to talk then, and I'm really looking forward to that. I already think you're an amazing guy, so I can't wait to get to know you better."

He shot me another reassuring smile. "Finally, you'll try to empty your bladder once more - as much as you can. And when you're done, I'll probably need to do one final in-and-out cath to make sure you leave here with an empty tank. Oh, and there's a little *bonus* surprise at the end if I think it's warranted - just one more mystery to keep you interested."

Corey paused once again to give me a mock-serious look. "Now, I'm about to ask you *the* dumbest thing that I'm required to utter: Do you have any questions or concerns?"

I blinked, trying to piece together everything he'd just said. "Um, well, I can see why my urologist was so vague. D'you think he'll press charges if I punch him during my follow-up appointment?"

I got a genuine laugh from my big, beautiful, um, nurse god? Wait, no! *Norse* God! Lurd. *Focus Ollie.*

"Seriously, sir," I added, "I'm trying to remember anything you said after 'prostate exam' and 'In & Out Burger.' Please tell me this isn't a closed-book test."

Corey chuckled again. "Nope, all open-book - and I'm

honored to be your cheat sheet. Now..." He gestured toward my clothes. "... let's get you out of those."

CHAPTER 5: LAYERS OF TRUST

Corey didn't miss a beat. He saw my hesitation and immediately offered, "Oops, my bad. If you're more comfortable peeing with your clothes still on, go ahead and do that first."

I nodded, grateful for his understanding, and shuffled up to the Bizarre Medical Experiments chair-table. I fumbled with my zipper, and a new dilemma hit me: *do I use both hands to get my dick out first, or hold the funnel in place with one hand while freeing myself with the other?* My brain decided now was the perfect time to short-circuit.

"Here," Corey's calm voice cut through my internal panic from behind me. "If you're being honest about not being pee shy, let me hold the funnel. You just focus on everything else."

His tone was so casual, so matter-of-fact, it almost calmed me. He didn't even glance down - just kept his eyes fixed somewhere in the distance while holding the funnel precisely where it needed to be. Before I could muster a "Thanks," he looked back at me with that same reassuring expression and added, "I'm a nurse. It's my job."

And he smiled. *Damn that smile.*

Taking a deep breath, I did my best to pee my heart out. Or at least every ounce in my uncooperative bladder. As predicted, I fell short of my expectations. After an awkward few moments of straining, I shrugged and stepped back as Corey returned the funnel to its hanging position. He noted the amount of liquid against the scale on the container then caught my concerned expression.

"There are no wrong answers on this test, Ollie" he said smoothly. "Now, let's really get you out of those clothes."

Cue my next blush.

I toed out of my shoes, unbuckled my belt and unzipped my fly. I let my pants fall to the floor. As I awkwardly stepped out of them, I suddenly realized I had no clue where to put them.

My benevolent Norse God Corey politely pointed toward a set of hooks on the wall back by the door. "Right over there," he said casually.

I felt his gaze as I walked over. I draped my pants neatly over a hook, took my socks off and laid them over my hanging pants. Then, taking a steadying breath, I decided to just go for it. I faced Corey, crossed my arms and pulled my shirt up over my head in one smooth motion.

Standing there, shirtless, in my undies, and definitely

feeling exposed, I waited for his reaction. Corey's expression didn't waver; if anything, his tone softened as he spoke. "Damn, Ollie. I'm not sure you need to get any bigger. Look at you." He smiled, genuine and warmly, before adding, "I might still slip up and call you 'my boy,' but make no mistake - you're a stunning man. And I'm probably gonna slip up again and repeat that your dad is an idiot. Because, Ollie... You are *every* proud father's dream son."

Oops, that hit me harder than I expected. I know he meant it as a sincere compliment, but my emotions were so raw today that another tear slipped out before I could stop it. Corey immediately noticed and looked devastated, like he'd just broken me. In an instant, I was wrapped in my second much-needed hug of the day.

"I'm so sorry, Ollie," Corey said, his voice full of regret. "I messed up. Here I was promising you I'd get you through this safely, and then I go and immediately make you cry."

"It's okay," I muttered, leaning into the warmth of his embrace. "Honestly, I needed the hug. The doctor told me I hold too much inside until things accidentally slip out. That was just a slip." I let out a weak chuckle. "Kinda like the problem I'm here for, right?"

Corey gave a thoughtful chuckle, and for a few moments, we just stood there. Me in my boxer briefs, him holding me like I was the most important person in the world. But as the moment passed, reality set in. Corey took a step back, and I instinctively slapped both hands over the front of my underwear, my face going pink all over again.

Corey's chuckle turned into a sweet laugh. "Oops, that's my second bad for the day. Don't worry - just pretend I'm your football coach, and you're stripping down to hit the showers."

"Uh, sir?" I stammered, my brain scrambling to keep up. "My coach isn't gay. I didn't have a crush on him. And he definitely didn't hug me so often. Wait! I mean, I didn't think he was cute. Oh, lurd - I mean, well... He wasn't about to give me a prostate exam!" I threw my hands up in defeat. *I give up.*

Corey's smirk was back in full force. "Well, I guess your, um, 'excitement' means you're getting a little more comfortable with me. At least for a second." He winked before adding, "Now, how about we take the next step? Off with the underwear, Ollie, and let's head to the table."

I meekly removed my shorts, feeling entirely too aware of myself. My dick was definitely still in the "fluffed" category, and it wasn't exactly moving toward the softer side of things. I'm not a typical "grower, not a shower" guy - I'm more of a 50/50 guy - but at this rate, I was dangerously close to proving just how much more I could grow *and* show. Oddly enough, though, I was starting to feel okay with it as I walked over to the far table.

Then Corey hit me with the most non sequitur question ever. "How flexible are you? Can you do a loose child's pose on the table?"

"I guess?" I replied, a little dumbfounded.

"Perfect. Okay buddy, hop up on the table and kneel facing the wall. Put your toes over the edge, and lower your front to your elbows. Like you're settling into a child's pose."

Exposed and intimate. Yep, I was definitely punching my urologist after this.

Corey's movements were calm and professional, but I hadn't noticed he'd already slipped on gloves and grabbed what had to be a tube of lube. As I settled into position, I felt his warm hand on the small of my back, and my breath hitched involuntarily.

"Easy, Ollie," he said in a soothing tone. "Here's what I'm going to do. It's all okay. Just like you do in your football stadium, I need to get familiar with my playing field. I'm going to do this exam for a few different reasons. First, I need to see what I'm working with."

There was a brief pause before Corey added, almost as an afterthought, "And dang, do you ever have the most beautiful playing field."

Ha! A small reprieve. At least with my head facing the wall, Corey couldn't see just how bright red my cheeks were. Well, at least the ones on my face.

"Secondly, I'll check for any external or internal hemorrhoids, and I need to feel your prostate, to check its size and firmness. Finally, I'll have you to get up, move to the chair-table, and I'm going to massage your prostate until you almost have an orgasm."

I let an "Eep!" escape before I could stop it.

Corey chuckled softly, his tone reassuring. "I promise, Ollie, it's nothing to worry about. I'll talk you through everything."

I felt his hand leave my back and move down my cleft. I think I shivered. I shouldn't be shivering - right? Except I was. It only got worse when I felt his thumb and index finger gently part my cheeks, right over my hole. I let out a sound that was somewhere between a gasp and a whimper.

"Sorry Corey," I squeaked out, my voice trembling.

Corey's tone was warm and gentle. "Ollie, no more apologies. You're doing fine. Like I said, this is a 'show your excitement' part of the test. Your body's natural reactions are completely normal. Just allow yourself to enjoy it. I get the feeling you need to let that happen a little more often than you currently do."

I tried to relax. I felt the cool gel touch my skin moments before I felt his gloved right index finger touch my hole. And I full-on gasped. The feeling exponentially more intense than when I had used my own finger. I prepared for the poke, but it didn't come. Instead, he just gently rubbed around my ring. There was something oddly soothing about his touch. And my face burned with embarrassment again.

"You're doing great," Corey said encouragingly. "Everything looks perfect so far - no signs of external hemorrhoids." His tone shifted into a playful tease. "Also, bonus points for having the most beautiful, furry, curly, blond taint I've ever seen. You're setting the bar high, Ollie."

I couldn't help but chuckle softly, with a mixture of nerves and relief. "Um... thanks? I think?"

He chuckled. "You're welcome. And hey, you're officially eligible for the first of our mystery surprises. But don't worry about that just yet. For now, just keep breathing and relaxing. You're in good hands. But, um, I'm sorry."

Wait what? "Why are you sorry?"

"Don't worry, just keep relaxing."

And I felt his finger push through my pucker. Oh my lurd. Frak. I've never felt anything so glorious in my life. I had always suspected that my butt could give me amazing feelings; I just didn't understand that it could give me such ecstasy. Oops, I think I just moaned.

"That's my boy. You're taking this like a champ. I'm going to push all the way in, and just stay there for a while. In addition to all I've told you, I also figured you'd probably be tight. This will help the probe go in much easier. Because, I maybe kinda forgot to mention, I can't use lube on it due to the tape and electrodes." He chuckled, "Hey, I felt that, don't tense up."

He was wrong for once. Damn, it felt so magical. I didn't tense, I just wanted to hug the finger that was my new best friend.

Back in his nurse mode he continued, "Okay, I'm going to start moving in and out and rotating my finger to feel for any internal hemorrhoids. With that lack of lube, I don't want to cause any bleeding. Hey, I felt that too. Relax."

He was right on that one. *Blood? Oh, never mind, who cares?* Feeling his finger gently sawing in and out of my butt was the new most amazing thing I've ever felt. *Please, never stop.*

I sensed his demeanor lighten again, "Hey Ollie, you're doing really great. I think I've finally found a way to calm you down and make you stop apologizing."

"I'm sorry, what? I'm having a hard time concentrating right now" I chuckled. I figured if he could joke, I should too. Until he smacked my butt.

I definitely tensed up and then he chuckled, saying "Now that's my boy." I just knew he was smirking.

"Okay Ollie, all good things must end… for even better things to start. Your rectum is as perfect as you are. I'm going to remove my finger, slowly, so don't tense up. And then I want you to carefully step off the table and get on to the chair table. Okay?"

I felt his finger slowly back out; I almost cried for a whole new reason. And then immediately had my next back-to-reality panic attack. Thankfully, Corey was way ahead of me "Ollie, I'm expecting you to be hard. Don't worry, we're doing so well. Just accept the attention. *Turn around and be proud!*"

Frak it, he asked for it, he assured me, I trust him. I think I even *need* him. I got off the table and turned around.

I understand that I had a thick, curly bush, but I had never wanted to tame it just to make my dick look bigger. Sure, I haven't seen that many hard dicks in person. While my soft one might get a bit lost in the bushes, I was satisfied that my erection towered above it. And I was pretty much towering at the moment. Forty-five degrees of little Ollie pointed at the sky.

"Ollie! Damn buddy. You deserve another very unprofessional moment. Your penis is just as impressive as you are. Oops, my turn to say I'm sorry. Size does not matter, but my boy, I hope you make that size count."

Forget "frak," I decided to switch to "Fuck." I couldn't blush any harder without causing a nosebleed. "I don't know if I make it count. Aside from my hand, I'm a little short on real world experience."

"No worries my man. It seems you have two amazing playing fields, front and back. Just be gentle and slow as you learn how to use them both. Okay, now keep that monster 'excited' and get up on the chair."

As much as I initially feared the chair/table/horror experiment thing, I kinda sorta felt excited to get on it. Corey seemed fine with my body and my erection. What's to fear?

Okay, wait! Awkwardness, definitely awkwardness!

That was the catch. My ass was barely on the edge of the "seat." My legs were all splayed out, and not all that comfortable. Suddenly I realized what "exposed" really meant. The ever-clairvoyant Corey placed his hand on my thigh and said, "I've still got you, trust me." He pressed a few buttons, and my back started to lower as my legs started to raise. Lol. More comfortable, but even more exposed. Then all movement stopped.

Corey jumped back in, "Here's the next level my friend. I'm going to use two fingers to stimulate and massage your prostate. I'm also going to find out exactly how far to insert that anal probe catheter. Finally, like I said, I'm going to do my best to get you so excited, you start expressing pre-ejaculate. Are you okay?"

"Sir, I have no idea. I'm so far out of any imagined comfort zone; I'm in the *Twilight Zone*."

"You really don't have to call me 'Sir,' unless it makes you feel more comfortable. And, wow, I'm almost too young to know what the 'Twilight Zone' is. I'm impressed."

"My father says, I mean, said, that I'm an old soul."

"Ollie... let's not think about him right now, I need you here with me. Because here we go."

I had already jumped over to using the word "fuck", right? "Frak" hadn't even cut it with one finger, let alone two. And I felt those two fingers on my hole, pressing in and up. And when I looked up, I was instantly trapped in Corey's caring eyes. "That's it Ollie. Prepare for Level Two, I'm going to go really slowly. Just keep looking at me." For the first time, I felt a burn as his fingers slowly sank in. He gently hushed me and assured me that I was doing good. And I like doing good.

Then it happened. Something I'd never imagined. An electric bolt of sheer joy and pleasure. Apparently, I can't hide any emotion, so of course, Corey instantly grinned and said "*That* my Ollie, is your prostate. I think he's about to be your new favorite body part. Thankfully, he doesn't seem to be too big or too soft. Let's hope he's not your current problem. So how 'bout you just let him be your current pleasure."

I couldn't help it, I let my head drop back as I focused on the most amazing feelings washing over me. And they just kept coming. Wave after wave. My lurd, I realized, my ass was going to forever rule my world. Until I had that sudden, urgent panic I guess all boys can get - especially when they're trying to avoid it. "Corey! Stop!"

To my surprise and disappointment, the pressure from his fingers immediately stopped and his fingers froze in place. He sheepishly smiled at me and said "That's my third bad. But that's exactly what I was about to tell you to let me know. You just got there a little faster than I expected. That's okay. Look down."

After I got my eyes to focus again, I looked at my dick and saw that I was leaking like, well, like a 19-year-old who just had his first life changing prostate massage. As I was staring, I involuntarily tensed and I swear, I kinda spurted out a little fountain of precum.

Corey let out a "Damn boy, good job. I don't care what the book says about procedure, this is going to make the next *not* fun part of the test so much less painful."

As he raised the chair back and lowered my legs, he continued on. "One more time, Ollie, remember, I warned you that this next part isn't going to be nearly as enjoyable."

How did this magic man do it? As I regained my

senses and looked around, I saw that there were new tubes and daubers on a cart that had magically appeared next to my legs - and I noticed he was putting on new gloves. While he was wiggling his fingers and organizing his new artillery, he casually asked his second non sequitur. "When's the last time you had a bowel movement?"

Oh. Come. On! You just almost massaged my prostate to my first hands-free orgasm and now you ask that? Damn! I have got to disconnect my face from my thoughts. Yay, another life lesson.

Corey remained calm and collected as always. "I had to change gloves," he explained casually.

I felt the color drain from my face. "Uh, sor... I mean, just before I got here, it's my normal routine." The words stumbled out before I could stop them.

"Ollie, remember what I said - nothing your body naturally does is your fault." His voice was reassuring, but it didn't stop my embarrassment from bubbling up.

Then, unexpectedly, he gave me a proud smile that could have lit up the room. "And good boy! You didn't apologize - well, at least not *all* the way. And, that's what I needed to know. Congratulations, you've just earned your *second* fabulous surprise."

Good? Was that good? I didn't have much time to overthink it, because Corey took charge again, his tone shifting back into his gentle command mode. "Right now, how about you put your arms up and clasp your fingers behind your head. That way I'll see any reflex you might have to protect your penis."

I hesitated. "Uh, I promise I won't move my hands to my crotch. And... well, I'm kinda out of deodorant right now, and I think my body's busy telling my pits to work overtime." I gave Corey a genuine quizzical look, "Also, why do you think I'm going to reflexively try to protect my... um, you know?"

Corey raised an eyebrow and chuckled. "Sorry buddy, no time for questions. I need to do this while your pre-ejaculate is still fresh. Besides, your pits are never anything you need to hide from me. Now, arms up! And, well, it's all because of what I'm about to do... right... now!"

FUCK! I had to fight every instinct to not immediately grab my dick for protection. "Ouch!"

"I know, I'm sorry, Ollie," Corey's tone was professional but apologetic. "That burn was the antiseptic I had to douse your glans with. You're uncircumcised, which is great, but it makes a thorough swabbing even more important. We don't want any stray germs getting a free ride to your bladder.

"The strange feeling you're about to experience, right... now, is your first in-and-out catheter. I'll give you a second to process it before the next step. You can lower your hands and maybe grip the edges of the seat - it's about to get worse."

And he wasn't kidding. The vaguely offensive discomfort quickly escalated to a sharp, sickening pain. I clutched the sheet covering the chair's edge and shot

Corey a look - equal parts shock and a plea for mercy.

"It's okay, Ollie. That was the catheter moving through your prostate. It's made it into your bladder now, and you did it. The worst part is over." His voice was calm, soothing, as though willing me to believe him.

I felt a twinge of betrayal, but I guess the sudden, and admittedly short, pain would have only been worse if I were expecting "something" without knowing exactly how bad it was actually going to be. With no other choice, I just tried to relax.

"Now... on to your next new, unnatural sensation. I'm going to drain your bladder, and no matter how hard you try, you won't be able to stop it. So don't try. And what's my favorite thing to remind you?"

I exhaled, forcing the tension from my shoulders. "Don't worry? Just relax?"

Corey smiled, "You are the best, my boy. Here it comes."

The sound of liquid rushing into the milk-gallon-like container was strangely satisfying. But dang! There was so much. It just kept flowing and flowing. I realized that I began to feel the most relaxed and comfortable that I had since my little altercation with the guys trying to break in to my Bronco. Lurd, I guess I really needed to pee!

Corey's reassuring face softened, and I caught a flicker of concern in his eyes. "Okay, Ollie, listen to me - don't stress, alright? It looks like you only emptied about a quarter of your bladder on your own."

My face must've fallen; he immediately stepped in. "It's perfectly okay. We're not jumping to any conclusions here. That's not my job. My job is to walk you through this, and most importantly... spring those two surprises on you." His hand rested gently on my shoulder as he added, "I'm here with you little brother. No worries, right?"

CHAPTER 6: FABULOUS SURPRISES

Corey leaned in with a reassuring smile. "Alright, Ollie, before we get to those two fabulous surprises, there's one last not-so-fabulous thing we have to endure. Just look at me and breathe, okay?"

I did, right up until the moment the catheter slid out past my prostate. "Gah! It hurts going out too?!"

"Yeah, sorry about that," Corey said, wincing sympathetically. "But it's all done. And hey, now you know what to expect next time. No more surprises there." He caught my look and raised a brow. "And no, my poker-faced boy. I see that look. You can't just bolt for the door."

I managed a shaky chuckle. "Corey, um… thank you. This is all way beyond 'intimate and exposed,' but somehow, you're making it bearable. Honestly, you've made me feel a lot more comfortable than I ever thought possible."

Corey put his hand over his face in mock shame.

"Remember you just said that, my beautiful, *furry*, boy, because here's the thing: for that probe tape and those electrodes to work, they need to be in full contact with your skin. And you, Ollie Otter, are rocking some serious furry real estate back there. Don't get me wrong, I'm furry too and I love it, it's wonderful."

I blinked. "So... What...?"

He smirked, but his tone stayed gentle. "I'm going to have to shave around your anus and most of your taint."

"Wait, what?!"

Corey held up a hand. "Hey - don't freak *yet*. There's more. Since you were so wonderfully honest about, er, admitting that you'd just had a bowel movement right before you got here, I need to give you a light enema before the shave."

My jaw dropped, and Corey instantly softened his expression. "I know, I know. I'm asking a lot from you, Ollie. But I promise, we're in this together."

I didn't need a mirror to know I'd gone pale again.

****

I was feeling totally out of control. Completely overwhelmed. And yet - ugh, I hated to admit it - maybe just a little... titillated?

"You okay, Ollie? I'm still here for you. You're still doing great."

I opened my mouth to respond, but nothing came out. What could I even say? Then the truth hit me. "Corey, I think I need another hug."

He smiled, another warm, unshakeable smile, and said, "Any time you need one, baby boy."

Wait. *Baby boy?!*

As he released me, I caught a glimpse of something different in his expression - was that a touch of *genuine* guilt? Before I could even ask, Corey sheepishly admitted, "Mary, our receptionist, told me how you reacted when she called you that earlier. I guess I'm up to my next bad, huh?"

I blinked, expecting to feel exposed or betrayed, but instead... I just felt loved. "I mean, I'm not really a baby, but I'm not feeling all that invincible today either. And, well, I kinda like the way you say it."

Corey leaned back away from me with a playful grin and said, "Let's get back over to the other table. Enema first. I swear, it's not that bad."

"Sure... says my 'trusted guide' who somehow forgot to mention what a catheter pushing through your prostate feels like."

Ooh, another butt-cheek slap. This one definitely made me understand that I kinda *really* liked them.

"I think we've established that you react positively to attention to your backside. You're gonna do just fine. Now just put your right knee on the table. And rest on your hands. Not your elbows. Try to stay mostly upright."

I glanced back, my nerves buzzing again as I noticed something new in Corey's hands: A bottle with a nozzle in his right hand, and I noticed a dollop of lube on his left index finger. I braced myself for the inevitable. I felt the cool sensation on my hole. After, what? thirty minutes, I was quickly getting used to it. And starting to just trust Corey.

"Alright, are you keeping count? Here's your next new sensation," Corey said, his tone light but grounding.

And it was. The nozzle slipped in with far less resistance than I expected, but the real surprise was Corey's left arm crossing my chest, pulling me gently but firmly back into his chest. "Stay upright for me," he simply commanded, his voice close and soothing. "I don't want the saline to go too deep; we're just cleaning your rectum."

The cool liquid began flowing into me - a *new* and strange but not unpleasant sensation. My mind, however, was more focused on the feeling of Corey's steady presence behind me, spooning me. The way he held me, his strength offering both support and comfort, was something I hadn't realized I needed so desperately. I just never would have guessed that this was how I would ever get it.

I closed my eyes, focusing on the flow of the cool liquid and the warmth of Corey's arm across my chest. I could feel myself growing hard again, my body betraying my attempts to stay composed. I silently begged my dick to not get too carried away this time.

"It's all in," Corey said after a moment, stepping back and releasing his hold. "Just stay in that position for a little while, and I'll be right here if you need me." His voice was steady, professional, and kind. As he moved to the sink, I exhaled, feeling both relieved and oddly comforted.

Then I chuckled to myself. I guess standing here, with one knee on the table, fully exposing my ass crack, with a rectum full of water, is par for the course today. I mean, it's nothing compared to almost having a hands-free orgasm from a prostate massage or the extreme discomfort of the catheter.

Corey walked back over to me and patted my shoulder. "Okay buddy, go sit on the toilet and expel the water."

Huh?

He gave me a kind, but stern look and restated, "I promise, I'll turn around; it's okay." He did and I took a seat. Everything came out as planned. And I didn't die of embarrassment. It was just water with a slight tinge of color. Corey judged the results and said, "Let's do it again, just one more time."

Once again, I assumed the position with my knee on the table, with my erection, now trapped under the table's edge. And Corey repeated his end of the process. Only this time, I actively leaned my back into his chest and let the back of my head lean against his shoulder. Was I taking advantage of the situation? Was I perverted? I didn't know, but again, I realized how much I'd missed physical contact with someone. And Corey wasn't protesting, in fact, he was holding me tighter.

"Okay, we're done, let that go, and then have a seat on

the table."

CHAPTER 7: MOWING THE PLAYING FIELD

I had no issues being nude, when it was my choice. I had solid pecs, mostly visible abs, a narrow waist, a nice dick and I love my blond body hair. But sitting on the exam table, waiting for Corey to gather whatever supplies he needed, and waiting for my erection to go down, I felt naked and exposed. I guess that was exactly what Dr. Rainer had warned me about.

Corey walked over before my cock could fully soften. He had a tube of something, a damp cloth, a dry cloth, a disposable razor and a pair of electric trimmers. Poof, erection gone. Once again, he read my emotions perfectly and gave me that mischievous half grin. "Don't worry, this is another *exciting* part. I promise, we'll make that beast hard again."

Before I could protest, he continued, "There are two positions we can do this in. Both are that 'intimate and exposed' thing you keep hearing about. First, we could go over to the chair table and I can raise and spread your legs and lower the back all the way down so that you're in what's called 'The Birthing Position.' Or we can stay here and have you get on your knees and elbows again. If you'll allow me to tell a bad doctor-dad joke, I call that, the position you got pregnant in. So, your choice: *give birth* or *get pregnant*?"

"That's a choice? Um, I guess, we can stay here."

"Good, it's actually a lot easier for me to see what I'm doing and be more exact in what I have to trim and shave."

"Then why didn't you just say that?"

"A lot of guys think it feels demeaning."

"Hey, demeaning is another new experience, right?" I mostly joked.

Corey replied seriously, "No, having your most private place shaved is the new experience, I'm not going to demean you, Ollie." Only to have his smirk quickly betray him, "Now, jump up. Put your head down and get your ass in the air. Boy!"

"Oh no, that's not demeaning at all, Sir." I was rewarded with another cheek slap as soon as my butt was up. I had hoped for it this time.

"Before I get started, Ollie, I have to say, you have the most beautiful butt crack I've ever seen on a 19-year-old. Your curled blond hair frames your little pink hole perfectly. What I'm about to do, should be a crime."

I have a pretty asshole? Again, that wasn't demeaning at all. Again, at least he couldn't see my blush.

"Okay," he began, his tone suddenly professional but still warm, "in addition to being a crime against humanity, shaving this part of a man's body is almost never recommended. The skin here is super sensitive, and even the smallest nick can lead to a serious infection.

"It's also prone to ingrown hairs when your natural furriness returns. That's why we did that little enema and why I'm using this special antiseptic shaving cream. But even with all that, you're getting another surprise. You'll need someone to check this area again on Monday or Tuesday; to reapply some antiseptic and make sure everything's recovering properly."

"Wait." My voice betrayed the worry bubbling up in my chest. "You said 'someone.' Won't you be here again?"

Corey hesitated just a moment too long, and I could swear there was a flicker of something - regret, maybe? - in his eyes before he replied. "Actually, I'm about 90 minutes away from home right now. I usually work at our clinic in Fort Worth, in the 8th Street medical district. I was asked to come here as a special request to perform an urgent urodynamic flow study for an important patient - you. This was the only clinic with availability to host the test anytime soon. I just assumed we were closer to your home."

His answer hit me hard. I felt a little too excited and maybe a little too giddy and said maybe a little too much. "Man, no! I'm 90 minutes away from home too! I usually stay in the South Hulen area, or near my LA Fitness on Westworth, close to Carswell. Is there any way I could see you at your 8th Street location?" I asked excitedly.

Corey's face turned into a smile. "Of course, Ollie, that's awesome. And what are the odds of such a wild coincidence?" His expression shifted, though, as he gave me a curious glance. "But, uh, what do you mean by 'usually stay in South Hulen *or* by your LA Fitness?'"

Frak. My heart skipped a few beats, and I scrambled to sound as nonchalant as possible. *Don't freak out. You're smart. Be chill.* "Ha, yeah, that was a weird way to say it. I guess it's my turn to have a 'bad.' I mean, I live on South Hulen, but after my co-op job, I work part-time at LA Fitness. So, you know, I'm just at both places a lot." I forced a smile, praying he'd buy it, but the way Corey studied me made me feel like I'd already slipped up.

His face didn't give me any clues, he simply moved back into nurse mode. "Cool, cool. Now back to the task at hand. I've seen this before with young guys who are still growing in to their adult hair patterns. Your cheeks are just lightly dusted with blond hairs, but your crack and taint are a real forest of fur. Again, it's a beautiful look. But I'm going to have to use the trimmers before I can use the blade. You already know what I'm going to say: Get ready for a new experience and a renewed erection."

Even though this position naturally caused my cheeks to part, Corey again gently used his left thumb and index finger over my hole, to push my cheeks even further apart. There was something about his care and tenderness that gave me an electric feeling and I couldn't stifle another shiver. Corey whispered, "It's alright. Here's the real treat." And the clippers clicked on.

I've used electric clippers to try to make my beard look as neatly maintained as dad's, well, and Corey's. And come to think of it, Dr. Rainer's. But my clippers suck and often pulled more hairs than they cut. I guess this pair was freshly sharpened or new. All I felt was the warmth of the little electric motor and a really pleasant vibration that at first, simply felt novel and a bit tingly, but soon grew to rock my world. I should always trust Corey. He was right, this is a fun part again.

I swear it lasted forever. His delicate, deliberate, moving of the trimmer. Adjusting his fingers and parting new areas of my cheeks. It was both mesmerizing and erotic. In fact, while the initial vibration, right on top of my hole, was wonderful, the further up my... did he call it my "taint?" he got, the more euphoric the feeling became. It was almost too late when I realized what the feeling was building up to and I immediately called out, "Corey! Stop!" for the second time today.

He did, and sounded concerned. "Oh no Ollie! Did I nick your scrotum? I was trying my best to make sure it was out of the way. Are you okay? I don't see any bleeding."

"No. Not that. I just realized that I was, um, enjoying it all a little too much. Remember my prostate massage?"

Corey gave a relieved chuckle. "I'm glad to hear that, Ollie. I'm almost finished anyway. Do you need a moment to calm down? Really, I just need a couple more strokes."

My sudden tension eased, "Nah, you can finish up, but I think I probably dripped all over your table."

Corey's chuckles continued, "It's okay. At least you'll be nice and lubed-up again for the sensor catheter."

Being forced to think about catheters again, quickly made my hard problem go away. I was fine for the next few buzzes.

The actual blade shaving was anti-climactic by comparison. Corey assured me the itchy regrowth over the next few weeks would *not* be one of the exciting parts.

CHAPTER 8: GOOD TO GO

"All shaved and good to go. Are you ready to finally start the actual test?" Corey gave a cheeky grin.

I replied in kind, "Oh, wait. There's more?"

That got a big smile from Corey. "Okay smart boy! Time to get serious. Back up on the chair. And sorry you lost your erection. But hey, the stiff catheter will at least make it look like you're trying." I saw my first Corey evil smirk.

I padded my way over to the table realizing how wrong my butt crack felt as I moved. As usual, Corey noticed my face. As well as noticing my face of realizing he'd already read me. "You're not my first furry patient. I know how 'wrong' your crack suddenly feels when you walk. Like I said, it's the worst thing I've done to you today. Since we now know we live close to each other, you can stop by my office any time and I promise I'll scratch your butt."

I wanted to slap *his* butt. Instead, I climbed into the chair-device, put my legs in the "stirrups" and once again put my entire crotch on full display for my Norse

God. The chair immediately started moving up as the back started reclining. Suddenly I knew exactly what Corey meant by "the birthing position." And I was in it.

"Hey?! I thought I chose the 'getting pregnant' position."

"You did *for shaving*. Now I gotta take advantage of all my hard work. This is only going to be slightly different from what we've already done. I'm going to insert the probe into your rectum and just gently nudge your prostate. Then I'm going to put the electrodes around your anus and finally, I need to tape everything in place. Just lie back and relax, you're prepared and you're going to do fine."

I relaxed my abs and let my head rest on the padded table. I immediately felt Corey's fingers around my hole and frak, I immediately started getting hard again. I'm definitely going to leave here with a bad case of blue balls.

Corey's command to take a deep breath, brought me back out of my head. I felt the probe at my entrance and I sucked my breath in. As the probe entered me, without lube, I was grateful Corey had "opened me up." I finally felt it gently nudge my new favorite spot.

"Are you okay Ollie? The probe is where it needs to be. Time to start taping things down."

He first attached the electrodes. I can't believe how much I loved having him just touch my bottom. And the taping? This needs to be a whole new kink thing. Well, I guess just having Corey touch my butt again, is my new favorite kink thing.

"We're all done down here. See? I told you we'd make it. And my best boy got hard again. I would *never* have expected that." Giving me his *second* evil smirk.

I needed to slap him. Face or butt - either one was good. Since I couldn't do either, I simply said, "Sorry *sir*," and smirked right back. His grin was genuine and bright.

"I'm proud of you Ollie, you adapt fast. I hate to bring it up again, but I feel sorry for your father. Everyone needs an Ollie in their life. You're an amazing guy."

I was glad my head was tilted back, out of his sight, but when Corey started turning the table back into a chair, he didn't miss the fresh tear tracks on my cheeks. His hand immediately and gently cupped my cheek once more.

"Okay," he said softly, his voice steady. "This is just another catheter. It's stiffer, but thinner. Here we go."

The strange sensation of something sliding into my urethra returned. It didn't exactly hurt, but it was far from natural. Corey's calm presence kept me grounded, and his warning came at just the right moment. "I'm at your prostate - hang on."

I braced myself, and thankfully, the pain passed quickly.

I expected another reassuring "You're done, good job," but instead, Corey's hands remained on my now only marginally deflated penis. Right! Taping, I'd nearly forgotten. I leaned my head back, trying to focus on the quiet efficiency of his ministrations. Somehow, our silence felt safe and reassuring.

When I glanced back down, my dick was neatly wrapped in what could only be described as a mummy costume. Corey gave me an approving grin.

"You, my boy, are ready to go," he announced, clapping his hands together with an almost theatrical flourish. His smile widened as he asked, "So! What are we gonna talk about?"

CHAPTER 9: A SOUL LAID BARE

After getting me all taped up and ready to go, Corey started the saline drip. He rolled his stool around to my right side, allowing us to have a conversation without my private parts being the center of our attention.

"This is the easy part of the test," he said with a grin. "And after ah, let me see, dang! 45 minutes, I think we deserve to relax a bit. I also think we're going to go over our allotted 90 minutes, but if you didn't pick up on it from earlier, you're my only reason for being here today, so I'm good. How about you?" Corey winked.

What did that mean? I decided to file it away for later and shrugged. "Everyone on my team *and* my manager told me they'd be very upset if they saw me again before Monday. I think they were trying to be sweet."

"Of course they were." Corey's voice softened with a sincerity that caught me off guard. "They obviously care about you. And we don't need to rush. This room is always booked in four-hour increments so facilities will have plenty of time for clean-up, even when a test goes long. So, we're golden. Okay?

He leaned forward, his tone turning professional again. "Here's all I need you to do. It's really simple: First, let me know the moment you feel the tiniest inkling of just thinking about needing to pee. Second, tell me when you'd start seriously looking for a gas station or rest stop if you were on a road trip. And third, let me know when you absolutely can't hold it anymore - within reason, of course. Other than that, your only job is to just chill." He ended with another mischievous grin.

Chill? Sure. *Totally. I'll just chillax right here!* I was stark naked, splayed out in what I now knew was dangerously close to "The Birthing Position." I had a probe up my butt, tape on my "taint" *and* penis; and a catheter slowly filling my bladder full of saline. All with my fantasy man seated right next to me, acting all casual like this was the most normal thing ever. Oh, and bonus points: I was also desperately trying to figure out how to get him to *repeat* all the "fun" parts of the test.

Once again, Corey pulled me out of my head as he said - and I swear - "I'm guessing you're the kind of guy who has an inner monologue going all the time. Am I right?"

I blinked and looked at him in stunned amazement, caught completely off guard. A nervous laugh escaped before I replied, "Your mind-reading skills are really starting to freak me out." We both chuckled, my tension eased slightly. I continued, "Yeah, but my inner monologue is being written by a noob who has no idea how to keep his thoughts straight or figure out where the story is going."

Corey raised an eyebrow, his lips transforming into his smirk that I was quickly learning to love. "Believe me, that's most of us. You're doing so much better than you think," he said, his voice kind but firm. "I mean, you've got to be under a lot of stress and have so many, well, unresolved emotions."

He didn't push further, though. Instead, he leaned back slightly, giving me space, and shifted the conversation. "But before we talk about any of that, I'm really curious: how does a 19-year-old land a job at a big company? A 19-year-old, who I'm assuming, hasn't graduated college yet?"

I appreciated the pivot, grateful for the chance to focus on something I actually liked talking about. If I didn't think too hard about my artificially erect mummy dick, this almost felt like just chatting with a coworker. "I'm a co-op student," I began, feeling even more at ease. "Most people are more familiar with interns, but there are some big differences. For one, co-ops start working after completing their first year of school and will have multiple semesters with their co-op company - interleaved with school semesters. And here's a big bonus! Co-op students are full-time employees while we're working, with all the benefits."

Corey nodded along, genuinely interested, and it encouraged me to keep going. "I think co-op students are most common in technical fields, like mechanical or electrical engineering. And me, I'm in software development - or at least, I hope to be. The big upside is that I'll graduate with over a year's worth of real-world experience. The downside? I'll graduate a year later than my peers. But honestly, I'm having such a great time, I don't care."

"That's so cool! So, you're just here for the semester? Like, from January until, uh, sometime in May? Then you head back to school for the summer?" Corey asked, tilting his head and raising his eyebrows with genuine curiosity.

"Nope," I replied, shaking my head. "I always seem to be a special case. Though, honestly, you're the only person who knows the whole story. I'm staying here until the start of the fall semester in September. Officially, it's because some key courses I need aren't being offered during the summer term."

"And unofficially?" Corey's tone sharpened; his attention locked on me.

"Unofficially, since my parents cut me off, I need to save up more money," I admitted with a small shrug, trying to sound nonchalant. "I'm lucky to have a nearly full-ride scholarship, but I still need to pay for a place to sleep, food, and, of course, textbooks. Talk about an institutionalized monopoly."

Corey let out a low groan. "Course books were expensive when I was in college - which wasn't even that long ago. But I can only imagine how much worse it's gotten." He paused, his gaze sincere and concerned. "Do you think you'll have enough to make it?"

"I'm going to try," I said with a determined nod. "The problem is, since I'm on a big scholarship, I can't just apply for a campus job. This is dumb, but my earnings would just reduce my scholarship and take away the opportunity for someone without scholarships to earn the money instead. It's weird, but I guess I see their point. Anyway, I'm getting pretty good at finding creative ways to cut my spending."

Corey raised an intrigued eyebrow, "Like how?"

"Well, like..." I started with a grin, "opportunistic part-time jobs off-campus. I mentioned the LA Fitness near where I work, right? I'm not qualified to be a trainer or anything, but I can be a gofer and, well, a janitor - *junior grade*," I added with a chuckle. "And the best part! I get to work out and shower any time I want. More money, free workouts. Win-win!"

"Ollie, my boy, you're one impressively resourceful pup. But why is showering so important? I mean, aside from keeping your wonderfully aromatic pits in check for a professional setting?"

I gulped. Did he mean anything by that question other than just keeping the conversation going? I stammered on, "Well, since the gym's close to work, it's easy to squeeze in an early workout before heading to the office."

Suddenly realizing I had an advantage, I replied, "But, wait... um, you like my pits? Is that what you just said?"

Corey's grin widened into the biggest mischievous smirk I'd ever seen - I loved it. "Hey, you're the guy who just got hard when I taped a probe up his butthole. So, let's not kink-shame me." That broke any remaining tension; we both burst into laughter.

"Alright," he started, still chuckling, "I'll admit, it might be a mostly gay male thing, but yeah - some of us appreciate the musk of a hot boy's curly blond pits. And yours? Well, they're absolutely man-candy material. Furry, fragrant, with just the right balance of 'woof' and 'mmm.'"

That made me laugh so hard I almost, *almost*, raised my arms over my head, just for him. But Corey wasn't finished.

"It's a very personal thing, though," he continued, tilting his head as if explaining a nuanced art form. "Even if you like a good pit scent, you probably won't like every man's. Oh, and even then, there's a big difference between 'sexy pit scent' or 'post workout bliss' and well, 'stressed-out pit odor' or 'dude, you need a shower.'"

"With all the times I've gotten you excited this morning; *you* got that *sexy pit scent* thang goin' on." He said with a hokey affectation. "Hey, it's just your body reacting to my rubber hammer." He winked. "And for the record, I like it. You kinda smell like you could be my little brother."

I must have had a deer-in-the-headlights look again because Corey leaned back in and said, "Did I hit a truth or two you're just now realizing?"

I couldn't help but laugh at his uncanny accuracy. "Okay, how do you do that?"

He grinned. "You're a wonderful *baby* gay, Ollie. Meanwhile, I've been practicing for a while."

I blinked at him, utterly caught off guard.

He immediately noticed my reaction. "Whoa, wait. I didn't expect to get a second 'I feel seen' look from you. What did I do this time?"

Yes! A win! I couldn't resist teasing him. "Wait - you mean there's actually a look I've got that you can't immediately figure out?" I gave him my most triumphant grin. "Before I explain... Seriously, is it really okay for me to talk about all this? I always thought it was just... me."

"Yes! Please, Ollie. Go for it. Just don't forget to keep me updated on how your bladder's doing, okay?"

"Oh. Wow, now that you mention it, I can feel something. But it's weird - like, more in my... uh, dick head? Does that count?"

Corey chuckled softly, his expression both kind and professional. "Yes, it does. That's exactly what we're looking for. Now, what were you about to admit?"

I hesitated for a moment, then decided to just go for it. "Well... I've never said this to anyone before. But I, um... I loved the way my father's pits smelled when he came home from work. It was comforting, you know? They smelled manly and strong and, well... like *him*. Please don't take this the wrong way, but when you hugged me earlier, I realized you smell a lot like he did."

Corey's face softened into the warmest, most understanding smile. "Hey, buddy, how could I take that the wrong way? That's probably the nicest thing anyone's said to me in a long time." His grin widened as he added,

"When I said you might smell like my brother, I meant the exact same thing in reverse. It's all good. Go on."

"And, I know this sounds like a total lie now - especially after, well, you having to shave me and all - but I was actually one of the last guys in my class to hit puberty. I've only been really furry for a few years now. I didn't have pubes or hair anywhere except my head until I was almost fifteen. Even my pediatrician was starting to worry.

"Honestly, I wasn't too embarrassed about it since I was already big and tall for my age. But I started obsessing over my classmates' and teammates' hair in the locker room. Especially their pits. To me, having pit hair meant you weren't just a kid anymore. And... I guess it's still a thing for me. Even now, after finally getting all the pit hair I could've ever dreamed of."

Corey grinned, a look of recognition sparked in his eyes. "Dayam, you really are my boy! I'm telling you; pit hair is the only socially acceptable kind of pubes a guy can show off in public. It's basically a badge of honor. So, yeah, I guess we're both sharing the same little kink." He gave me another teasing smirk. "But what did I say that made you give me that *second* 'I feel seen' look?"

"Oh, this is a bit more, um, hard-core, is that okay?"

"Ollie, of course it is. As long as it's alright with you."

I hesitated but found myself trusting Corey. "So, when I was 12, and still totally hairless - duh, I spent a summer week with my 15-year-old cousin. He was so *not* hairless. His bush and well, his more mature endowment, totally enthralled me. I was obsessed. I tried to see him naked as much as possible the whole time we were together.

Corey nodded, his expression understanding and encouraging.

"And finally, because he was enjoying my hero worship, he, well, not only let me look at and touch everything I wanted to, he decided to show me what big boys can do with their dicks. I just stood there and watched him jack off. When he came, I was a bit, ah, scared, I guess? But he explained how awesome it felt and that I would be able to do the same thing really soon and then I'd understand.

"Given I'd also expressed interest in all things butt related, he added that a really cool thing he and his friend did, was what he called *practicing*. In his words: 'Well, it's like practicing for real sex with a girl. We take turns putting our dicks up each other's butt. And the wild part is, having their dick in your butt, feels just as good as putting your dick in theirs.'

"That completely blew my 12-year-old brain. And I instantly realized I wanted to be practiced on. But, not to prepare for having 'real sex with a girl.' I knew I wanted to just be with another boy forever."

Corey gave me a knowing look, his tone tender. "And that's when you started figuring things out?"

"Yeah, I'm definitely condensing my realization, but that's when I knew I was probably gay."

Corey's smile deepened. "Buddy, when you decide to

open up, you go all out. I'm honored you shared that with me. Did you ever get to, er, *practice* with anyone?"

I instantly returned to my new-normal blushed state, "Ah, no. I just got to the mutual masturbation stage with a couple of friends. I was never brave enough to push for more. And well, I never felt like they wanted to as much as I did."

"Hey, that's fine. At least you got to get naked with a friend or two for fun. How's the bladder?" He asked, his tone light but with a professional undercurrent, effortlessly slipping back into nurse-mode.

I took a moment and checked in with my body. "I'm really close to looking for that gas station or rest stop. But it's more like only just thinking about it."

Corey glanced at the saline bag; its slow drip was gently emptying into my body. He nodded, seemingly satisfied that everything was progressing as expected. It was so strange - I couldn't physically feel the water flowing in through what should definitely be an "out hole." It just felt like a slow, natural buildup of needing to pee.

He gave me a new look: concerned, kind, and patient. "So... do you want to talk about your parents? I totally understand if you don't."

My gaze dropped back to my exposed crotch, as if searching for courage in the vulnerability of the moment. I let out a deep breath, shoulders sagging slightly. "No guarantees, but I can try. If you really want to hear it."

Corey leaned forward once again, his voice softening. "Hey, remember, we're best friends for the duration. No pressure, just an open invitation. I'd love to know more, if it feels right for you to share."

I glanced up into his genuinely concerned eyes and decided to continue. "So, my mom is great, but I've always been super close with my father. Sure, most boys think their dads are their super-heroes when they're kids, but with us, that feeling never really changed. I always thought of him as my best friend.

"When I started worrying about how all my friends had already gotten 'hair down there,' and I hadn't, I wasn't embarrassed to talk to him about it. He just listened, assured me that I was my own normal, and helped me wait it out. When my turn finally came, he supported me all through puberty.

"The funny part is, once I finally started getting hair, he gave me this whole big speech: 'Oliver, if you ever start feeling uncomfortable hugging me, it's okay. We can switch to shaking hands instead.' I immediately rejected his offer and hugged him harder than I ever had before and swore that nothing would ever make me not want to do that. I loved him. I couldn't imagine that changing.

"Of course, we had our differences. He loved watching my football games, but he always warned me not to let it interfere with my grades. He's a very devout church man, but after weeks of long debates, he eventually accepted that I'm not. And, he never questioned why I didn't date. He just appreciated my hard work -

both academically and on the field.

"So, when I started thinking about telling him I'm gay, it didn't even cross my mind that he wouldn't accept it. I figured he and Mom probably already knew. Even *I* thought it was pretty obvious by that time." I flashed a quick smile to Corey, "I mean, you pretty much instantly figured it out."

My smile vanished just as quickly, replaced by reflective regret. "I let myself believe that telling them would lead to one of those heartfelt, affirming *Family Hug of Acceptance* moments, like I'd seen on TV.

"But, um." I stumbled, "I was an idiot. I was totally blindsided by their reaction. It was all so sudden and severe; it knocked the ground out from under me. There were no questions. No 'we still love you.' Just..." my voice cracked, "well, what I told you before: 'Here's what we're giving you. Now get out of our house by tomorrow morning.'"

"I uttered two, simple, desperate words: 'But Father?'" I took a shaky breath, the memory still cutting deep. "Then he *hit* me. He backhanded me hard enough to knock me to the floor. My nose even started bleeding. I was so shocked, I couldn't even cry. My father had never ever even spanked me before. Not once. I was in total denial that this could really be happening. It was like my whole world had been shattered in an instant."

I paused, my voice trembling. "I numbly packed my clothes and some personal stuff and shoved everything into my Bronco. I left before the sun was completely up. No one came out to stop me. No one came to say goodbye. I felt like I was comatose - just sleepwalking through the motions.

"It wasn't until two or three hours later that it all finally hit me. I suddenly had to pull over on the freeway shoulder and throw up. Everything came crashing down at once. But even then, I still couldn't cry. Not really. I had too much to face ahead of me."

I made the mistake of looking up at Corey's eyes. They were glistening, his expression was full of so much empathy it made my chest ache. That was it. My dam had finally broken. I started sobbing, hyperventilating, ugly crying in a way I hadn't since... well, *then*. Corey didn't hesitate. He pulled me over into his arms, holding me like I might break apart if he let go.

And I let him. I buried my face in his scrubs, soaking them with my tears. He didn't say anything, just held me for so many, wonderful, long minutes, like he knew that was exactly what I needed.

I finally started to calm down. Until...

"Corey! Stop!" I guess that seemed to be my go-to phrase around him. It was ironic because I had never once actually wanted him to stop anything he was doing.

He pulled back slightly, concern written all over his face. My pained smile returned him to the present. "I'll need you to finish that hug later," I uttered, embarrassed but desperate, "but right now, my bladder is about to burst. I'm seriously about to pee myself again."

Corey's lips twitched with a gentle smile as he brushed his fingers along my blond baby beard. "Got it, my bad. And…" He gave a playful wince. "I think I've lost count. Okay, I'm going to stop the flow, and we need to get back to the test."

His touch, his tone - everything about him - made me feel like I wasn't just a bundle of nerves and embarrassment anymore. I was starting to feel… safe.

CHAPTER 10: BROKEN TRUST

I was right on the edge of hurting, and Corey could tell. "Alright, Ollie, I know you're totally full, but we need to knock out two final quick things first. They're easy, I promise. You're an athlete, so you've heard this before. Turn your head to the left and cough. I'll be watching for any leakage. Go ahead."

I did as he instructed and was sure I leaked. Corey gave a small nod, confirming what I already knew. I instinctively started to turn my head the other way, and before he could say anything, I coughed again.

His eyes lit up with a playful glint. "Look at you, reading my mind now."

Despite the pressure building in my bladder, I couldn't help but feel a tiny bit of satisfaction at his approval.

"Alright Ollie, we're in the home stretch," Corey said, his tone reassuring. "But once again, I've got a new sensation for you to process. The catheter in your penis is thin enough that you'll be able to urinate around it. If I did my job right - and trust me, I always do - you can just pee in your current position and everything will flow into the funnel and down into the measuring container. You just need to relax and let it happen."

He paused; his expression still caring. "I know you're not pee shy, but this time I'm going to give you some privacy. I'll turn the faucet on for inspiration and step out for a few minutes to take care of some administrative items. I also know this is an awkward break in our conversation, are you going to be okay?"

There he was again, making sure I was more than just physically fine. It was like he could see through every layer of me, down to where I was feeling raw, terrified and alone.

I nodded, maybe too quickly. "Seriously, I'll be fine. So, I just need to sit here and pee, right? I can handle that. I promise."

He smiled; his warm, effortless smile made me feel safe in ways I hadn't realized I could feel anymore. Corey turned the faucet on, the sound of rushing water filling the room, and then he slipped out, leaving me alone with my thoughts and, well, my assignment.

For a moment, the aloneness felt too heavy again. I let out a shaky breath and maybe, a tear or two slipped out before I could stop them. But once more, I pulled myself together. I had a job to do, and for once, it wasn't even anything overwhelming or confusing. It was simple. I closed my eyes, focused on the sound of the running water, and did my best to let everything flow out of my body.

To my surprise - and immense relief - I didn't get that dreaded, embarrassing warm feeling of urine trickling down across my balls and through my crack. Instead, I heard the distinct sound of liquid dripping into the plastic container. Success! I kept focusing on relaxing as much as possible, just letting the flow take over. But it stopped way sooner than I hoped.

Come on... I'd just gone through thirty minutes of being filled with saline while baring my soul to Corey, and it only took like fifteen seconds to drain? *That can't be right. Er, right?*

Determined to make it work, I tried pushing hard. Nothing. I flexed my "taint" muscles - and, let's be honest, "taint" has become my new favorite word - but still no luck. I even hesitated, wondering if I might mess up the sensors if I tried any harder. But I knew my pressure to urinate wasn't gone. It felt like there was a lot more left - refusing to come out. But I guess my body was finished.

Before I could spiral down into a full-blown panic attack, Corey walked back into the room with his usual calm energy. "So?" he asked with a playful smirk. "Everything come out okay?" He barely paused before adding, "Sorry, occupational humor."

"I don't know," I admitted, feeling another wave of anxiety creep up. "I think I'm done, but I might've tried too hard and... I'm worried I messed up the sensors or something."

"No worries Ollie. That's exactly why the sensors

are in those places your body never wanted them to be. Well," he added with a mischievous grin as he lightly tapped the anal probe, "except maybe this one." My nearly strangled dick gave the slightest, traitorous twitch.

He laughed softly at my obvious embarrassment and leaned back slightly. "Ollie, you are so many things. First off, you're definitely my favorite patient. Probably ever. You're honest, sincere, resourceful, and strong. And, unfortunately, you're also very consistent."

I blinked, unsure where this was going.

Corey glanced at the container and back at me, his tone professional again. "I know how much saline went into your bladder, and I know how much you just managed to expel on your own. The amounts are almost identical to the numbers you gave me at the start."

The weight of his words settled in, and I couldn't help but take it as a failure. My stomach sank, my chest tightened, and I felt the newly familiar sting of disappointment bubbling up. I've never been good at dealing with failure, and I was clearly losing this battle now too.

Of course, Corey saw it all written on my face - I guessed that's his super-power. His voice gentled even more as he leaned closer. "No, Ollie, listen to me. This isn't a failure. It's not even about failing or passing. It just means there's something preventing your bladder from emptying the way it should. That's what we're here to figure out, together. You haven't failed anything."

I wanted to believe him. I really did. But the words felt hollow, like they weren't meant for my personality type. Until Corey continued.

"This test is going to give your doctor a lot of important information," he said, his tone shifting back into nurse mode. "And all we want it to do is confirm that everything is perfectly fine with your bladder, pelvic muscles, prostate - the whole shebang. But..." He paused, and there it was: his reassuring smile, sadly sliding into a remorseful shrug. "I'm definitely going to have to do that second in-and-out cath I mentioned. And we know that's not exactly a new sensation for you at this point."

I sighed. "Can't wait," I said dryly.

His mischievous smile made a slight comeback, "Hold on, buddy, because first..." He paused dramatically, raising up a small bottle of liquid like it was some kind of holy relic. "I have to do some new, very mean, things that I *kiiinda sooorta* forgot to mention earlier. If they're too bad, I'll let you punch me."

"How generous of you," I muttered, already dreading whatever was coming.

Corey's grin remained unfazed. "So, you know how it feels when you rip a band-aid off? Now imagine that - *times ten.* All your areas that I've had to tape up? Well, they're super sensitive. Removing the tape is going to be... *memorable.*"

My sudden trust in this man may have just lost some traction. "Can't we just leave it on and let it... I don't know, wear off naturally? Hey, I could maybe start a new fashion trend."

Corey chuckled, appreciating my half-hearted joke. "As tempting as that is, *nope*. But! If you promise not to hit me, I've got this near-magical tape glue solvent that makes it about ten times *easier*. So that puts us back to nearly even. Sound fair?"

"Do I have a choice?" I snarked, shrugging in reluctant acceptance.

"Great!" Corey said cheerfully, clearly ignoring my resignation. "Let's start with the bottom first."

I suddenly felt the sensation I'd been dreading while trying my best to pee around the catheter earlier. My butt was getting wet. Then came a gentle tugging sensation. Like all the strange things Corey had done to my bottom today, it was weirdly... *not unpleasant*. I even kind of liked it - *again.*

Corey started a play-by-play. "Okay, that's most of the tape. Now for the electrodes... done. And finally, for the probe. Going... going... out!"

Wait. Is it bad that I missed the feeling of it being inside me? No time to overthink because Corey was already moving on.

"Sorry Ollie. That was the easy part. Now for the serious part," he said with a faint, apologetic smile. "You've got two options: put your arms over your head - which you know is my preference - or grip the chair edge. But you need to pick one."

I hesitated, then decided to make him happy. Raising

my arms felt like an act of surrender, but if it made this easier, I'd do it. Corey smiled, and for a second, I let myself smile back. Until...

His first tug on the tape sent a penetrating, sickening pain radiating from my dick, through my balls, and up into my gut. I sucked in a sharp breath and yelped.

"I know, Ollie. I'm so sorry," Corey said, his tone soft but firm. "I have to keep going. Just grab the top of the chair if it gets to be too much."

Frak! This hurt like nothing I had ever experienced before. Corey needed to get his hands away from my dick - now! I was seconds from telling him that I'd handle it myself when he did the most non sequitur thing imaginable. He leaned forward, pressed his face into my right pit, sniffed it, and then - wait - was that a kiss? Or a lick? My brain short-circuited again.

Forget the pain. Forget *everything*. My world zeroed in on the surreal, electric sensation of having Corey's face in my pit. For one fleeting moment, everything in my world felt... *perfect*. Like my whole universe had just snapped into place.

But then he leaned back, looking sheepish, holding up a wad of wet tape and the catheter like they were trophies. "See? All done. The tape's off, and the catheter sensor is out. I knew that would distract you." He smiled, but with a guilty flicker in his eye I didn't understand. "You can still punch me in the shoulder if you want to." He added unnecessarily.

My euphoric haze shattered. My head spun with

confusion, embarrassment, and something I couldn't name. I just sat there, staring at him, utterly at a loss for words.

Corey's smile faltered. "Was that too much? I thought we were at a point where we could handle a little off-script distraction during a painful moment. Did I mess up?"

My mouth was dry, my thoughts were a tangled mess. I finally managed to mumble, "Uh, no. It helped... I think? Exactly like you... um, intended, I guess." My voice wavered. "Do you... normally do that with your patients?"

He laughed, but it sounded forced. "No, Ollie. I just thought it was appropriate for our situation." He hesitated, then added, "Though I've been known to pinch a nipple before."

I didn't laugh. My mind was still stuck on figuring out if this was all just a scripted trick to get me though his test.

Corey cleared his throat, his tone back to his most professional. "Look, it's all about building trust and understanding during this long, emotional, and yes, embarrassing test. I wouldn't have done that with any-one else. Are we still okay? Because we've got one last thing to do, Are you ready?"

His words hung in the air, waiting. I couldn't answer yet. I wasn't even sure how I felt.

CHAPTER 11: ALL THAT I HAVE

Damn. Why did Corey suddenly sound so professional and weirdly aloof? Did he really just kiss my pit *only* because he knew it would work as my perfect distraction? Was I letting myself imagine way too much? Everyone warned me about this test being "intimate and exposed." I seemed to keep understanding what that means on whole new levels, like, well, every 20 minutes.

"I see you writing your inner monologue again." Corey's voice was softer now, but pensive. "Don't write an ending yet. We're still here. We still have more to do. Are you still with me?"

"Yes, sir," I replied, unable to keep a hint of sarcasm from creeping in. I regretted it instantly, but the words were already out.

Corey's face fell, just slightly. "Ollie, that's not what I meant. I swear, I'm not playing you. I'm trying my best to help you through this. I promise."

The sincerity in his voice caught me off guard, but my embarrassment was still bubbling under the surface.

"Okay," I muttered, quieter this time. "I'm sorry. I really am. I just… didn't expect any of this today."

Corey's gaze shifted; his expression unreadable. Then he said, almost too quietly, "Believe me, Ollie, I didn't either."

Nonplussed again. Damn it.

I let a shaky breath out, nodding as I relaxed just a little. "Yeah," I said, my voice steadier now. "I'm ready."

Corey studied me for a moment, then gave a slight nod, his expression changing into something I couldn't quite place. "Okay, my man. Once more into the fire."

I couldn't help but cringe at the phrase, but to Corey's credit, I really did know what to expect. And maybe, just maybe, it didn't hurt as badly this time. Or maybe I was just a little numb.

****

After my bladder had been drained, I thought I was done. I figured all the fun parts, the awkward parts, and the painful parts were over. I was sure I'd accidentally made us both end on a dour note. But Corey wasn't finished.

"My brave Ollie," he began, his voice steady but more solemn than before. "Remember back at the start, when I told you there might be one last surprise? But only if I felt it was warranted?"

I nodded; my curiosity piqued despite myself.

"Well," he continued, "please trust me one last time - it is warranted. Under typical circumstances, I'd tell my patient to go home and, well... masturbate as soon as possible. It serves two purposes: it flushes out everything the massage stirred up in your prostate, and after three catheters, it soothes your urethra. And yours definitely needs soothing."

I blinked, unsure how to process what he was saying. Corey must've noticed my hesitation because he pressed on, his tone more persuasive now.

"Plus, my man, you've come so close to climaxing twice this morning, and you've got at least a 90-minute drive ahead of you. That's blue balls just waiting to happen." He gazed into my eyes, nothing mischievous about it this time. "So... will you let me help you, uh, relieve the pressure? I swear, Ollie, you need it."

For once, I wasn't shocked. I was too exhausted to be. Instead, I just gave him a wry smile and replied, "Nah, I'm good."

And I started to get up.

But Corey gently placed his hand on my chest, stopping me before I could fully rise. "Ollie, please trust me," he said softly. "I've only been trying to learn everything about you this morning because I like you and care about helping you - not to trick you or embarrass you. Please, don't just leave like this."

I let out a long sigh, my shoulders slumping under the weight of everything I'd been feeling. "Corey, I think I've said too much already. I've confessed things to you I've never told anyone else. And your explanation for kissing my pit made me feel a whole new level of exposed *and embarrassed*." I paused; the words I wasn't sure I wanted to say already forming in my mouth. "Because the truth is... I think I've started to fall for you. How stupid is that? It's like I've regressed to some ridiculous tween-age crush." I shook my head. "I just need to go. I need to be alone for a while. I'm sorry."

Corey's expression shifted; his warmth replaced with something stronger - a quiet determination. Before I could turn away, he gently cupped my cheeks with both his hands, the touch grounding me in place. He leaned forward until his inquisitive eyes locked with my heartbroken ones, not letting me escape.

"Don't be sorry," he said, his voice steady but filled with an unshakable sincerity. "But... I only have one more question before you leave, and I need you to answer me honestly. Ollie... where exactly is your home?"

The breath caught in my throat, and my heart pounded. How did he know? How could he see through me so completely, when I'd spent months hiding this from everyone? My defenses crumbled under the weight of his question, and for the second time today, I broke down completely. Sobs wracked my chest, and I barely managed to choke out the truth.

"I live in my car!" I cried, my voice shaking with the rawness of my admission. *"It's all I have!"*

CHAPTER 12: ALL OUT CONFESSIONS

Once again, I found myself in Corey's big arms, crying into his chest, breathing in his scent, hoping it could anchor me - begging it to comfort me. For the second time this morning, I felt completely broken, my composure was shattered into so many pieces I didn't know if it could ever be put back together.

I pulled away, leaning back into the chair. "I'm just so lost. I don't understand anything anymore." My voice weak, barely audible. "I don't know what's real, or what I'm imagining, or what I was trying to wish into reality. Corey, I like - no, I'm sorry - I think I almost fell in love with you."

I couldn't look at him as I spoke. My words tumbled out, raw and jagged. "But I get it now. All your kindness and caring... that's just part of your job, right? To make people feel comfortable during a really 'intimate and exposed' test. But I - I started reading a lot more into it than I should have. You've made me realize how much I miss having a best friend, a big brother, a dad - just... *someone*."

I forced myself to take a shaky breath, ignoring my tears that were threatening to fall again. "And I really need to leave now. Because I know that *someone* can't be you. It's not your fault, it's mine. Please, sir, I just need to go."

Corey resumed our hug and his arms tightened around me, holding me in place. "Ollie," he said softly, his voice steady but tinged with something I couldn't yet determine, "listen to me. There's so much you don't know. So much I probably - no, *definitely* - should have told you sooner."

He leaned back just enough to make me meet his gaze, his hands firm and warm on my shoulders. "Let me start with my confession. If you think you were 'juvenile' for *slowly* falling for me over two hours, imagine how childish I felt when I started falling for you *at first sight*."

I blinked, stunned, my mind racing again to catch up with his words.

"When I opened the waiting room door this morning and saw you - this big, beautiful boy who was trying so hard to be brave, but was so obviously terrified and alone - I felt instincts sharper than I'd ever felt before. I wanted to grab you, hold you close, take you home and protect you forever. From then on, the more you shared with me, the more I knew my first impression was right, and the more I found myself completely falling for the amazing person you are.

"Ollie, everything we've done today has been 100%

legit, but I couldn't stop myself. I knew it was professionally, well, *risky*, but I had to give you all the comforting touches I could - more than I've ever given a patient before. I've even lost count of all our full-frontal hugs. I don't usually, okay *ever,* do that. And by the way, no - that was not a normal rectal exam or prostate massage. I mean they were *mechanically* correct, but I knew exactly what I was doing. I wanted to make sure you enjoyed it. I wanted you to feel the extra care I was putting into it.

"And it wasn't just that. I hope you felt the same with - sorry - the enema. You're absolutely capable of staying upright on your own without my arm across your chest. But I... I wanted to hold you. And I thought you wanted to be held, too.

"When I kissed your armpit, Ollie, yes. I was trying to distract you. But I can't lie; I loved it. And when I saw that you did, too... I realized I might've crossed the line from risky over to *dangerous.* I lost my nerve and tried to blow it off like it was nothing. Please believe me when I say this: I've never, *ever,* pinched another patient's nipple." He chuckled lightly as his cheeks flushed a soft pink.

"Then I saw the shift in your eyes, and I realized I'd done something far worse than crossing a line - I made you feel betrayed. Or at least tricked. And I panicked. I couldn't let you leave like that. From the little slip-ups you made during our conversations, I had a strong suspicion that you didn't have a real home to go back to. And I'm so, so sorry for asking you that awful question when you were at your most vulnerable. I only did it because... because I hoped it would make you stay long enough for me to recover from my mistake.

"Ollie, yes, I like you. More than I should probably admit. I want to be your friend, your big brother - or something more, if that's what you'd ever want. But whatever it may be, I just want to be here for you *now*. Please forgive me?"

Tears were streaming down my cheeks once again, but they had changed. They weren't sad anymore. Instead, they were hopeful - almost happy. I wiped at my eyes, failing miserably, and said the first dumb thing that popped into my head: "Buddy, when you decide to make a confession, you go all out."

I chuckled through my tears and leaned forward to hug him in tight, wrapping my arms around him like I'd never let go. For the first time, I felt my need echoed in his embrace - like he'd never let go either. I noticed a few tears on his face too.

CHAPTER 13:
THE FIRST KISS

Corey leaned back, straightened up, sniffed his tears away, and with a small but reassuring smile, Nurse Corey had regained control. "Ollie, I know I might be pressing my luck here, but I'm serious. You're still very naked, and you still need to, well, have a release. I can leave the room and let you handle it on your own, or I can stay and help give you the ending you deserve. It's totally up to you, but you're not leaving here without having an orgasm first."

He chuckled softly, a hint of nervousness making him even more endearing. "And here's one more confession - there's absolutely no way this is a standard part of the test." His grin turned playful. "Except for a couple of *very* unintentional accidents, I've never helped a patient have an orgasm before. I mean, I do give them the same speech I gave you, about why it's important. But then I send them on their way. And they are. On. Their. Own."

His expression brightened; his voice suddenly inviting. "So, if I may... Would you like to follow me back over to the exam table, one last time?"

I was back in his care again. "Yes sir!" I replied; my dick was already hard and enthusiastically pointing the way. I tried not to run over to the padded table at the back of the room.

"Are you ready to take this to the *next* level, my boy? Just hop up and lie back with your knees bent up. I think the best way I can help is by tickling your new favorite body part with one hand, while my other hand finds its own kind of mischief. All while you s-l-o-w-l-y take matters into your own hand. There's no need to rush this, you deserve to savor every feeling you're about to experience."

I jumped on the table and lowered my back down onto its padding, I raised my knees and looked over at Corey. I was hard as a steel pipe and was already worried that my dick was going to rush our time whether Corey wanted to or not.

I saw him get the tube of lube again and start slicking up two fingers on his right hand. And I involuntarily uttered, "Um, aren't you going to use a glove?"

"The test is over Ollie. I'd really like to touch you with my bare hands if you're okay with that. And before we get too much further, do you want any lube for your part of the task?"

I grinned, "Nope, it's one of the joys of being uncircumcised."

Corey returned to the table with a nearly predatory smirk, "Okay my boy, raise your knees to your chest and show me your playing field one more time."

I did, only this time, I didn't feel like I was simply exposing myself to Corey. I felt like I was offering myself and inviting him in. My anticipation was off the charts and I was starting to shiver again.

Then... everything stopped when I felt his fingers finally touch my expectant hole. I whimpered and involuntarily raised my bottom to better greet his fingers.

Corey gave me a corrective look, "Easy Ollie, I said we're going to take it slowly this time. That way we can do new things, like this..."

His face quickly changed into the most passionate smile. He kept his fingers firmly on my hole as he moved his body closer to mine, leaning over me. Face to face. His eyes silently asked the question I was longing to hear. And my eyes screamed "Yes!" in return. He lowered his head and our lips touched for the first time.

Every kiss I'd ever had before simply vanished into nothingness, erased in an instant. This will forever be my first kiss. His beard brushing against my skin, his scent enveloping me, his breath merging with mine - it was all-consuming. I wanted to cry out, overwhelmed with pure joy. But all I could do was let his probing tongue part my lips exactly at the moment his two bare fingers slid past my resistance. I moaned into his mouth, and pushed my hips up even higher, to make his flingers slide in deeper.

Corey eventually broke our kiss and gazed into my eyes. "How are you liking our new level my beautiful boy? Before you answer, consider this..." As his fingers finally connected with their target.

My enthusiasm exploded, but my words were primitive, "Damn! Please, just *never* stop Corey. Ever. Oh my god! Um, I have no idea why I ever said 'no' to you."

There was a trace of regret in his always kind eyes, "Because I accidently upset you. And I promise that I'm *so* going to make it up to you."

Corey unexpectedly slipped back into nurse command mode, but with a playful twist: "You can lower your feet back to the table now Ollie, I'm where I need to be. And how 'bout you raise your left arm please. Oh, and feel free to continue your task with your right one." He raised an eyebrow, "but remember, *slowly*."

I happily complied. As soon as my blond pit curls were again in his view, Corey leaned back down and nuzzled his nose in as far as he could. There was no quick sniff and lick this time. I reveled in the prolonged sensation and was almost on the verge of overstimulation.

He took a deep breath and then started sensually rubbing his chin and beard all up, down, and around my pit.

Forever the mind reader, he slowly moved back over my face and seductively said, "It's the best part of having a beard. I'm scenting it with my Ollie's musk. Now I'll never forget it." As he kissed me again, I could smell my scent on him. Damn. My joy was racing up so many new levels.

As overwhelmed as I was, there was absolutely no way I could coherently express any of the new desires rushing through my overloaded mind. So, Corey did it for me. "My Ollie, there are a lot of things I can't do here, but if you'd like, I can at least make this a little less one-sided."

I just nodded to his offer and started involuntarily quivering once again. But then immediately almost let a word of protest slip past my lips as I felt his fingers slide out of my playing field.

He caught my confused look, "Shhh, no worries my boy, they'll be right back. I just couldn't do *this* without leaving you untouched for a second." With that, Corey faced me like I had faced him hours ago. He crossed his arms and quickly removed his scrubs top.

He gave me a sheepish grin, his voice quiet but playful, "Sorry, I can't remove my bottoms. At least not here. We'll have to save that level for a more appropriate place." My Norse God stood there, modest smirk intact, as if waiting for my approval - a living, breathing masterpiece offering himself to my gaze.

I froze, caught in the now-familiar spell of Corey's presence. Somehow, I managed to stammer, "C-Corey! You're... beautiful. You're, um, like my fantasy man - *times ten.*"

His smile brightened into something even more radiant, and his voice carried a warmth that melted the last of my worries away. "Aww, I'm honored. Just understand Ollie, I'm never going to slap you to the floor, and I'll always be here to hug you, no matter how old you get." Joy exploded from my chest, filling every corner of my soul.

Corey was a work of art. His dark blond fur, slightly thicker and deeper in tone than how I remembered my father's, framed his broad, rounded pecs perfectly. A triangular treasure trail disappeared into the waistband of his scrub bottoms, the soft lines of his tummy fur enhancing the hard ridges of his abs. And his pits - dark, damp, and utterly intoxicating - radiated masculinity. In that moment, I knew: I had found a new home. Or at least, I was about to feel truly safe and protected for the first time since fleeing mine.

He leaned back over me with his fingers gently yet expertly returning to their playing field. While I thought he was about to resume our kiss, instead he raised my left arm back up over my head and planted his tongue firmly in my curly blond tuft. Heaven again. Except he wasn't done, he maneuvered *his* left pit so that it was over my face. And I instinctively accepted his offer.

I dove in. His scent was grounding it was a bit like me; and yet it was still all Corey. And just like our kiss, I will always remember my first time of being offered this man's scent. It's indelibly stamped into my brain. As I continued to lick and suck and sniff, it was as if we were, well, I guess, 69-ing each other's musk makers. And in doing so, creating our own unique combined scent.

Once again, I was overwhelmed and said those two most contradictory words, but gentler this time with less urgently. "Cory, stop - *please*. Just for a second. I don't think I can hold off much longer, and I really want to be kissing you when I cum."

He smiled at me and softly said, "Your wish is my command." We laughed at the cheesiness until his fingers suddenly got even more serious with my prostate and his lips reconnected with mine.

As my pressure built and my stroke speed increased, I once again had to hold back tears from running down my cheeks. It didn't matter, because just three quick breaths later, and both Corey and I had something other than tears streaming down our cheeks. Or maybe that should be "gushing." I shot all over our beards, my chest, my abs and finally, just dribbled into my bush. Would it be redundant to say that my first shared climax had also just wiped all prior orgasms from my memory?

Corey's fingers slowly slipped from my soul, but his lips remained on mine as we both continued reveling in my post orgasmic bliss. But as I came down from my high, I started giggling - uncontrollably. Wait, what?

I finally managed to calm my giggles and give Corey a sheepish grin. "I swear, that was so incredible and so not funny. I mean, it was the most amazing thing I've ever experienced. But I'm just well... *happy*. I haven't felt this good, this carefree, in... well, since *you know*." My voice trailed off, but the joy in my chest was undeniable.

With a tenderness that made my heart sing, Corey gently brushed his fingers through my hair. "I couldn't be happier either, Ollie. And trust me, we've only scratched the surface. There are so many more levels for us to explore together."

He paused in realization, giving me a funny-but-pained smile. "But right now, we need to clean up and get out of this room before someone starts knocking." His hand lingered on my cheek for a final moment before he reluctantly pulled away. "Just lie there, my beautiful boy and catch your breath. I'll grab a washrag. You've got a lot of little baby Ollies in your beard - and, well, just about everywhere else. I was right, you definitely needed that."

CHAPTER 14: SUPER MARIO CART

I waited in my Bronco as Corey pulled around in his car. Dang - a Mustang Mach E! My man is *electric*. It's funny, I always thought the EV Mustang looked like a muscle car in its third trimester, but now? Seeing Corey in his, I've reassessed its merits. It's officially the coolest car on the planet. And of course, it's the most appropriate chariot to carry my Norse God. He parked next to me and strolled over to my window.

"Ollie, now that I've found you, please don't let me lose you," he said with a half-smile that was equal parts playful and sincere.

I beamed and held up my iPhone. "No worries, I've got Google Maps. Where are we going?"

"It's almost lunchtime, and I'm guessing neither of us had breakfast this morning." His eyes danced over me knowingly. I didn't feel the need to admit I hadn't eaten dinner last night either, so I just nodded.

"Cool. Trust me on this, put '4434 Harry Hines Blvd'

into your phone. Got it? Show it to me - let me see." LOL, he definitely wasn't about to lose me.

"Awesome. It's a little place called the Original Market Diner. It's a real diner so we can decide whether we're feeling more like breakfast or lunch when we get there. And Ollie..." He paused, his tone turning serious, "don't overthink it too much, but, we *really* need to talk. Just... not on empty stomachs."

I gave him a questioning look, "I promise I won't, but um, can't I just follow you?"

"Of course you can - that's the plan. But this is Dallas traffic. In case anything happens and we get separated, I want you to know where we're going. And duh! We need to exchange contacts while we're at it."

We began our maniacal Super Mario Kart race straight into the heart of Dallas. Back in Michigan, I'd always done my best to avoid Detroit craziness for all my driving life, but Dallas and Fort Worth traffic made Detroit look absolutely sane. Between reckless drivers - Turn Signals? We don't need no stinking Turn Signals! - and random unexplainable pockets of construction - oh and even a freaking car on fire - it really was like driving through a video game freeway obstacle course.

During rare gaps in the bumper-car chaos, I caught a few glimpses of downtown Dallas. The city had a big, brash, boldness about it. As if it was something whose only reason for being, was to be huge and impressive. Through it all, I managed to keep my eyes glued to Corey's sleek EV taillights, determined not to lose him either. I breathed a sigh of relief when we finally entered the tiny parking lot of our little diner - undented and unscratched - and found two open parking spots.

CHAPTER 15: EVERYONE NEEDS AN OLLIE IN THEIR LIFE

As soon as we stepped out of our vehicles and reconnected, Corey pulled me into another hug, completely unconcerned with the world around us. For a moment, I stiffened. I don't know... doing this so boldly and out in the open was really new to me. I felt almost embarrassed - or at least a little self-conscious. I know Corey felt my concern. He confidently looked into my doubting eyes to reassure me, "Ollie, it's all okay. You don't need to hide anything anymore."

He smiled and quickly returned to the task at hand, "Let's go get some food, and I'll try my best to explain everything you don't know - in a way that won't leave you feeling embarrassed, exposed, or tricked again."

I raised an eyebrow and retorted, "You do understand that *you're* supposed to be the *older and wiser* one, right? So, you gotta know that wasn't your best opening line."

I gave him a chance to see my mischievous grin before continuing, "This place better have some amazing food to make up for it." His face registered a hint of respect at my attempt to recover from my little blunder.

We walked across the parking lot toward the diner, as I took it all in. This place was like stepping into a time capsule - like episodes of *Happy Days* had never ended. Or better yet, like they'd been real all along. The wait staff inside were either 50's-era moms personified or, well - gay. And at least a few of the tables had couples or groups that were pretty obviously gay too. Hey, maybe that was what the '50s were really like - just hidden under its *happy* surface.

The hostess led us around a display of rotating pies, past the register and into a second dining room. And finally gestured to the last booth on the left - back by the far wall of the building. As soon as we slid in and opened our menus, Corey gleefully switched into big brother mode, recommending his two favorite menu items. One if I wanted breakfast, the other if I was leaning toward lunch. The breakfast option - something called "Sam's Benedict" - sounded really delicious, so I ordered it, *plus* a side of pancakes. I was absolutely starving.

As she took our orders, our waitress - definitely one of the "moms" - was clearly trying to figure out exactly what Corey and I meant to each other. I couldn't blame her. Heck, I was trying to figure that one out myself.

Corey waited until our "mom" left, before leaning across the table, his gaze kind but serious. "Okay, my Ollie, you've had forty-five long minutes alone in your car. I know that overthinking brain of yours has been hard at work, writing lots of new inner monologue. So... how are we doing?"

I let out a breath I hadn't even realized I'd been holding and relaxed. "Hey, you're the one who keeps dropping ominous hints about things I don't know. You've already ripped two painful band-aids off me today. Could you maybe just *please*... rip this one off now too?"

"Fair enough." Corey's expression turned solemn, his hands resting on the table between us. "So, remember earlier, when I asked you that awful question? The question I already suspected I knew the answer to?" His voice caught slightly, and he cleared his throat. "God, Ollie, I'm sorry I had to do that. And you... well, you said, '*It's all I have.*'" He paused, his voice trembling just enough to let me know how deeply my revelation had affected him.

"Ollie, please don't get upset. But your Bronco isn't even *close* to being all you have. While we may have just met in person this morning, I've actually known about you for a lot longer."

My eyes were threatening to get real damp again, and it kind of looked like Corey's might start dripping as well. I swallowed hard and gave him a small nod to urge him to continue - unsure if it was really what I wanted him to do.

Corey gave a weak smile and attempted to lighten the moment. "Hey, instead of raising your arms above your head this time, maybe you could just hand me your car keys?"

Without thinking, I actually started to. He chuckled softly but didn't take them. Instead, he just firmly held my hands over the table.

"Ollie, I don't think you realize the kind of impression you leave on the people you meet. You deliver an impact that makes everyone instantly *deeply* care about you. Your whole team at work absolutely adores you. They see your talent, your kindness, and your determination.

"And believe me, they've been watching you, and *worrying* about you. They knew you were going through some really tough times. So, they kept trying to find ways to get you to ask them for help. But apparently, if there's one thing you *don't* do well, it's to admit when you need it. Which, in its own way, makes them care and worry about you even more.

"They don't know the full story of what happened during your fight, or even why it happened. I think I've figured some of it out, but that doesn't matter right now. What matters is that the fight's consequences gave them the opportunity to intervene with your personal life. It gave them an excuse to *care* for you the way you *deserve*.

"And, Ollie..." Corey hesitated for just a moment, his tone more serious than ever. "I don't know if you've thought about it, but you've never asked me about my last name. It's been on my scrub's name tag all morning, but I'm guessing you've had, well, you know, other things on your mind."

He gave a small, nearly playful smile, "So, my brave boy, here goes your last band-aid: Hello Oliver Carson, it's been amazing getting to know you this morning, I'm Corey Rainer."

I froze. My mind buffering the unexpected details for several seconds before their understanding hit me - harder than the pain from tape being ripped off my most sensitive parts earlier this morning. My breath caught. "Wait - you're Dr. Rainer's son?!"

"That's right my boy - yes. And as I've asked you to do so many times today, please don't freak. Just let me explain. And, well... maybe *really*, give me your car keys." Corey winked, flashing an impossibly sweet smile; it worked.

It was more than enough to keep me from bolting up and out of our booth. Then again, I wasn't entirely sure I could *bolt* anyway. Lurd! Why was everything so tiny in this quaint little place? Was everybody really that much smaller back in the '50s? Or - was this why Corey brought me here, to trap me in a nostalgia-filled cage where I couldn't make a quick escape?

Corey fixed me in his gaze once again as he continued. "Here's the whole story. My dad - your urologist - isn't just a good friend of your mentor, Ted. They've been a couple for the last 20 years and married since 2015. So! What that means is, right now, you're sitting across from the result of my dad's one and only *'practice'* with a real girl." He punctuated his revelation, "See? I really have been listening to everything you've shared with me today.

"Dad and Mom tried marriage for a while, but it wasn't the right thing for either of them. I mean, they both loved me very much, but they also knew that staying together wasn't going to make anyone happy in the long run.

"Like you, I've always been my father's son. I love my mom, and I got to see her as often as I wanted, but my dad was - and still is - my world. So, when you told me your story, Ollie... it shattered my heart. I cried because I could imagine exactly how devastating it would feel to lose that connection.

"Unlike you, I had a happy ending. When I came out to Dad, he just hugged me, laughed and said, 'Well, I guess you got all my best genes. I love you son.' That's what you deserved to hear too - the simple acceptance and understanding from the person you loved and needed most."

Corey pivoted slightly, realizing he may have accidently given me a new cause for concern, "And please don't worry. You haven't been outed to anyone you're not ready to tell. No one on your team knows you're gay - though, believe me, none of them would care. They all just think you're the greatest co-op they've ever known. But 'Uncle Ted' - yep, that's what I call him - strongly suspected it and yes, he knows for sure now. That was kinda unavoidable."

Corey paused, watching me closely. "You're awfully quiet, but you don't look like you're going to faint or flee. Are you okay?"

I let out a shaky breath. "I have no idea. I can't figure out anything to say yet. So... what else?"

"So, it was a no-brainer for Ted to send you to dad... Er, Chris... Ah, Dr. Rainer. And when it became clear that you needed this test, they asked me to step in. They trusted me to take care of a boy they had both gotten to know and love."

I blinked hard at the word "love" but stayed silent.

Corey continued; his reassuring baritone keeping me calm. "I was supposed to do the test and discreetly get as much personal information out of you as I could. They both suspected you were living in your Bronco, but they wanted me to confirm it. So that they could help you.

"I agreed to their plan, but what I never imagined was that I'd immediately fall for you too. At first, I was just trying to get information - to help you and do what I'd promised. But after only our first few minutes together, everything changed. I suddenly *needed* to know every-thing about you - not because I had been asked to, but because I realized I cared so much about you.

And, in a strange way - even for today - I knew I had to earn your trust. In fact, it became the most important thing for me to do. Yet I still came so close to blowing it, and losing you. I'm so sorry my Ollie."

His look saddened until he paused and regrouped.

Corey's voice grew more confident and he straight-ened up. "Ollie, what I'm trying to say is - again - your Bronco isn't even close to being all you have. You've got a whole team of people at work. You have two new dads, well, maybe *granddads* - don't you *dare* repeat that!" His mischievous grin had returned. "And you've got *me*. All of us care about you and will always be here for you, whenever you need us.

"Congratulations, Oliver Carson. You've managed to ace the hardest test this life has ever thrown at you." He reached over and gently cupped my cheek. "Like I said, everyone needs an Ollie in their life. Please, be in ours... Please be in mine."

I didn't think my insides could melt any more than they already had today, but they absolutely did.

CHAPTER 16: LEARNING TEXAN

Even after such an amazing moment, Corey smoothly shifted back into his mischievous mode. "Oh, and just so you know, Dad and Ted have already set up a room for you at their place. I think you'll like it... it used to be mine."

"Wait, what?" My jaw practically hit the table. "You're telling me all of this... Pulling me into this... This amazing new world, and I'm supposed to just accept it *without* winding up with you?"

Corey leaned back, his soft chuckle was warm and disarming. "Ollie, my boy, this isn't some fantasy porn story. There's no way we get to just skip ahead to living happily ever after together. We have to be real; I just turned 29 and you're only 19 - fine *almost* 20 - but still in school, and just now starting to figure out what being gay means to you. I care about you way too much to rush into anything and wind up putting unnecessary pressure on you to figure everything out all at once."

He gave me another gentle, knowing smile, "Remember how embarrassed you were - just a little while ago -

out there in the parking lot? You're still learning Ollie. And that's exactly what you need to do, you just need space to do it.

"When I stepped out of our room earlier this morning for those 'administrative items' - while you were trying to pee, I gave Dad a call. I filled him in on how everything was going and, I gave him the rest of the story from my car on our way here. He's as shocked - and *thrilled* - as I am about what's happened between us. But his dad genes roared into overdrive. He's already laid down the law. And honestly, I can't disagree with him.

"Ollie, you're so new to all this and so vulnerable right now. You've been through so much abuse recently. None of us - me, Dad, Ted - can bear the thought of you being hurt any more. I know it might be hard to understand, but moving in with me, *right now*, would probably only add more stress to your life. And that's the last thing I want for you.

"Believe me, I want to be with you. I want to *learn* you, to give you everything you deserve. But if we ever have a fight - and we will because even the happiest couples do - I don't ever want you feeling like your only option is to go sleep in your Bronco again. I want you to have a safe place, one that's *yours*, no matter what's happening with *us*.

"Please don't doubt what happened between us today. It was real. It *is* real. I haven't felt this way about someone in... well, ever. But we're not on equal footing yet. I need to make sure you'll always be okay, Ollie, even if -" his voice faltered, as his sky-blue eyes sought reassurance from mine, "- even if we don't work out. I need to know that you'll be safe." His smile quickly returned, "And if you're wondering? Yes. I'm hoping with all my heart that we *do*."

"While we're exploring *us* and figuring out exactly what *we* are, I want you to be safe and secure with Dad and Ted. I'll even spend the weekend with y'all to help you settle in. And don't worry, I only live a neighborhood away from your new home. We'll always be close. So, Ollie, will you make it official: *mi padre's casa es tu casa*. Si?"

I rolled my eyes, "Corey, I'm from *Michigan*. I don't speak *Texan*." I managed a genuine, carefree chuckle, my first one in what felt like forever.

When I was unexpectedly banished from my home three months ago, I'd never felt more lost and alone. I thought back to my exodus down I-69 - getting sick along the side of the road, realizing I had no idea what to expect and no one to turn to. But now, on this unimaginable morning, I regained something I thought I'd lost forever: People who cared about me. People I could be good for. People I could make proud. And maybe, people I could love - and who would love me back.

A long-forgotten, but welcome feeling washed over me.

"Corey," I said, suddenly laughing at the absurdity of it all, "where's the restroom? I really, *really* need to go pee."

Corey's face lit up with his trademark mischievous

grin. "It's just right over there. That's my boy!"

A PERSONAL NOTE

Thank you for reading Ollie's Test. This story means more to me than I can fully express, and I'd like to share why.

When I was a couple of years older than Ollie - fresh out of my co-op program - I had an experience that left a lasting mark on me. During what I thought was going to be a routine physical, a doctor crossed a line. It wasn't violent or forced, but it was deeply inappropriate, and I didn't know enough to recognize it at the time. I was naïve, trusting, and completely unprepared for the humiliation that followed. When the inevitable happened, the doctor laughed at me. I left the building in tears and didn't see another doctor for over a decade.

Years later, a psychiatrist friend gave me an idea: take that moment and turn it into fiction. Reclaim control. Rewrite the narrative so that, instead of shame and helplessness, the main character could find strength, protection, and understanding.

Then, just a few months ago, I underwent the same urodynamic flow study that Ollie experiences in this book. The nurse performing it - a kind, middle-aged mother of two - confided in me that late-teen and early-20s boys often struggled during the procedure. Many became overwhelmed, some broke down in tears. I suddenly found myself reliving my own past, but this time, I had an outlet. I had an Ollie. And I had a Corey - Ollie's champion and protector - to make sure the story played out the way I wished it had for me.

That's why I wrote this book. I had to. I needed Ollie to have someone in his corner, and I hope his journey resonates with you as much as it did for me.

Thank you for being here,
Mark